# THE BILLIONAIRE'S SCANDAL

JEANNETTE WINTERS

## Jeannette Winters
## Author Contact

website:
JeannetteWinters.com
email:
authorjeannettewinters@gmail.com
Facebook:
Author Jeannette Winters
Twitter:
JWintersAuthor
Newsletter Signup:
www.jeannettewinters.com/newsletter

### Also follow me on:
BookBub:
bookbub.com/authors/jeannette-winters
Goodreads:
https://www.goodreads.com/author/show/
13514560.Jeannette_Winters
Pinterest:
https://www.pinterest.com/authorjw/boards/

# DEDICATION

*This book is dedicated all my friends, new and old. I treasure each and every one of you.... HUGS.....*

*Karen Lawson and Janet Hitchcock my editors you are amazing!*

*To my readers who continue to inspire me with endless messages and kind words. Always make time for romance.*

# THE BILLIONAIRE'S SCANDAL

Trust was something Gareth Lawson had little of lately. His family means everything to him, but lies and deceit threatens to crumble them from within. He's not going to sit back and wait for the next ball to drop. It's time to turn the tables and take back control.

Brooke Cortes lives her life the way she wants too, one happy adventure after another. Who wouldn't want to see the world, one country at a time? The only commitment she has, is to live life to its fullest.

Although Brooke and Gareth find themselves on the same tropical island, it is evident they were there for entirely different reasons. Tempers flare but so do the sparks. Yet their night of passion, almost turns into tragedy.

Has Gareth's drive for justice put Brooke's life in danger? Can he keep her out of the scandal that threatens his family? She trusted him with her heart. Now he has to prove to her that love heals all wounds.

---

Gareth Lawson looked at the file. "Are you serious? That's . . ." He couldn't even bring himself to verbalize what he was reading. It stirred something in him that, for the first time in his life, he actually could kill.

"This is not even all of it. We could keep digging, but at this point, I wasn't sure you wanted to know. Hell, if this was my family, I know I wouldn't."

"That's you," Gareth responded, not lifting his eyes from the paper. "What will it cost me to have you dig deeper, to get everything?"

Roy shook his head. "I hate to break it to you, Gareth. I like working for you and everything, but this is the Hendersons we're talking about. I pushed my luck even getting this. The repercussions could be . . . well . . . really fucking bad. I'm sure this is something they would be willing to do *anything* to keep from getting out."

He could see why. Being connected to a human trafficking ring would definitely put a nail in the coffin. Gareth would normally let it go, but what Roy didn't know, was why that was important. If the Hendersons weren't related

JEANNETTE WINTERS

to the Lawsons, then fuck it, let them deal with the mess they made for themselves. But there was no way Gareth would allow this type of shit to attach itself to the Lawson name. They might not be perfect, hell, not even close, but this was beyond anything even his family would've done. *At least I hope so.* One sad fact he'd learned over the past year: the Lawson legacy wasn't everything they thought it had been.

Gareth pulled out his checkbook and paid Roy the agreed amount. He knew pushing Roy wasn't going to do any good. He saw the . . . fear maybe . . . in his eyes. Roy might have come highly recommended for fact-finding, but he had no balls. Gareth wouldn't have backed down from the Hendersons, not from anyone actually. *And that's why sometimes you've got to do it yourself.*

He handed Roy the check and stated firmly, "As per the terms, this information remains confidential, understood?" He didn't believe Roy would run his mouth but wanted to give him a reminder anyway.

"Trust me; I am beginning to wish I never took this job in the first place." He got up and, before leaving Gareth's office, turned back and said, "I hope you're not foolish enough to continue with this. I have a feeling if you do, the cost will be something you can't cover, even with a blank check."

Gareth was beginning to wonder if Roy actually had more than he'd shared. Something had him scared. The Hendersons weren't cold-blooded killers, yet Roy was acting as though they could be. Digging was exactly what Gareth planned to do. There was something about Tabiq no one wanted to talk about. The Hendersons were investing a shitload of money into that country. They said it was to make amends for something their father James had done. The question remained: how involved was James in what had taken place? Was he

2

just an investor? That was bad enough, but his gut said it went deeper.

Even though Roy never mentioned Gareth's great-grand-dad, he figured it was only an oversight.

Brushing the file to one side, Gareth growled, "This would be a lot fucking easier if Brice would've told us." He had two choices: be more persistent with Brice and demand that he tells him everything or continue on his own. *Until Brice figures out I'm not going away so easily.*

Gareth knew his kid brother, Dylan, would've pushed too, but Dylan was like a sledge hammer. He knew Dylan could've gotten it done, but the clean-up was another story. This wasn't like going after Maxwell Grayson. The skeletons in the Henderson closet were tied to the Lawsons. And this wasn't about taking the Hendersons down either. Knowledge was power, and Gareth wasn't about to leave his family powerless.

There were a few positive things going on that provided the family some much needed distraction right now. Little Penelope seemed to have everyone's attention, and if they weren't talking about her, they were talking about Dylan's child, the one on the way.

Gareth still couldn't believe Dylan was going to be a father. Hell, he thought for sure Dylan and he would be the last holdouts. The change happened so fast that Gareth never saw it coming. Their wedding was taking place in a few weeks and Gareth was avoiding anything to do with it. Even though Dylan said it was going to be a small low-key event, Gareth knew better. No way was Sofia's mother going to sit back and let that fly. So he shut his mouth and waited for the bomb to drop. Holding back his laughter when it did would be difficult.

They were all close, but he and Dylan especially so.

Maybe it was because they were so similar, or at least they used to be. Dylan now went home after work for a home-cooked meal while Gareth went out for a drink alone. At least it started that way, but now there was always some woman looking for him to buy her a drink. He looked up at the clock and it wasn't even noon. He had quit working that early before, but he needed answers more than a drink right now.

Since he wasn't about to include any of his family in this matter, he needed to make it appear that everything was normal. They wouldn't be shocked to learn he was taking a week or two off without notice. Gareth had built a reputation as a playboy, one he lived up to quit nicely. His brothers might not like it and grumble, but no one would care if he was gone, as long as he was back for the wedding. If his research was going to take more than a few weeks, they all had a bigger problem than he suspected.

He picked up his phone and knew who to call: Seth. That was the one person who would give him the least amount of grief. Seth wasn't much of a talker; he'd get to the point and keep moving. He was one of those guys who enjoyed his office job. Seth could spend hours reviewing a contract, and if anyone could find the minutest discrepancy, it was him.

If it wasn't for the fact Seth would freak the fuck out, Gareth would've loved to utilize his skills right now. But Seth would never agree to suck information from the rest of the family. So he was on his own. It probably was better that way. If anything went wrong, he was prepared to take the blame.

*Good thing, because I'm the one doing it.*

"Gareth, if you're calling me for an early lunch, you know my answer," Seth stated. "I'm in the middle of—"

"Yeah I know. A contract." *What else is new?* "That's not why I'm calling. I'm heading out of town for a few days, maybe more. Yeah, probably more. You know how it is."

"For some of us, yes I do. And you're calling me instead of Charles because . . ."

"He's probably tied up." *And will ask too many questions.*

"I'm glad you feel as though my time isn't as valuable. But don't worry, I'll pass along the message like usual," Seth said sarcastically.

That was usually when Gareth would come back with some snappy remark, but he didn't want to prolong the call any longer than necessary. "Thanks, Seth. And we'll do that lunch when I get back."

Seth grumbled, "I won't bother telling you to have a good time. One of these ladies will trip you up and you'll find yourself settled down, just like Charles and Dylan."

Gareth laughed. "I'm not sure you're reading a contract. It sounds more like a comic book. Mark my words, Seth, this guy isn't falling for any batting eyelashes or sweet voices."

"I wish I was a betting man. I'd gladly take your money," Seth said. "Now if you don't mind, I do have work to do."

Seth ended the call, and Gareth had to admit Lawson Steel was lucky to have him. That kind of dedication was exactly what was needed to drive the company forward. Of course, what they didn't seem to understand was it also took someone like Gareth to ensure nothing from their past jumped out and bit them in the ass.

Slipping his phone in his pocket, he closed his laptop and left the office. Normally he'd call their pilot to fuel up. But he didn't want anyone to know where he was going. Not now at least. If things got out of hand, maybe he'd come clean.

*For now, let them think I'm lying on a topless beach somewhere enjoying the view.*

Gareth couldn't help but wonder if New Hope Resort had such accommodations. He didn't believe it was the Hendersons' style, but their business partner, Drake Fletcher, was a gambling man, and Gareth had no idea what he was like. *But I'm about to find out.*

Brooke Cortes's hands shook as she wiped the frozen piña colada from the man's suit jacket. "I'm so sorry. I didn't see your suitcase there and I . . . oh . . . I'm so sorry." If things weren't bad enough, as she tried wiping with one hand, she continued spilling the drink with the other. "Really, sorry."

The man snarled. "Clumsy idiot. You should be fired. Where is your manager?"

*Fired?* That wasn't going to go over very well with her parents. They told her this was a dumb idea, but grabbing a job as a waitress in a fancy resort sounded like what she needed. Why had she thought it would be stress-free and allow for hours at the beach? *Because like you so kindly pointed out, mister, I'm an idiot, that's why.*

"If you'd like, I can have him paged," Brooke stated. She really hoped it wasn't going to come to that.

"That's a bit drastic, don't you think?" a deep voice said from behind her.

Brooke wanted to turn and see who it was, but the angry man in front of her held her attention.

"Do you know how much this suit cost?" he asked.

"I'll buy you a new one if you promise me one thing." She held her breath and waited as the mystery voice continued, "You apologize to this young lady for being such an ass."

The man's chest puffed up and his face turned beet red. "Who the hell do you think you're talking to?"

"A bully. And I don't like anyone who throws their weight around. For the record, I don't give a shit if you're the pope or the president, she deserves a bit of respect."

6

This wasn't doing her nerves any good. The two men now glared at each other. "I can't believe you dare speak to me in such a manner. I assume you work here as well."

"Hardly. I'm a guest. So, do you want the suit or are you just willing to walk away and go about your day?"

Brooke wasn't sure what the man was about to do, but eventually he huffed, grabbed his bag, and walked away. Only then did she turn her full attention to her rescuer. She instantly understood why the other man backed down. The guy looked fierce. She wouldn't have wanted to cross him. And from his tone, she knew he'd been prepared to back up whatever he said with action.

"You didn't have to do that, you know, but thank you." She did appreciate his assistance. She knew he'd have asked for Mr. Fletcher. Brooke hadn't been at New Hope long enough to anticipate how he'd have reacted to such a complaint. Mrs. Fletcher, on the other hand, didn't seem to get flustered over anything.

"The guy probably needed some cooling off anyway. My name is Gareth, and you are?"

"Brooke. I haven't seen you here before. Are you just checking in?"

"I am," he replied.

She smiled and said, "Welcome to New Hope. I'd shake your hand, but as you can see, I'm a bit sticky right now."

"Don't let that Neanderthal ruin the rest of your day."

She laughed. "He wasn't *that* bad." *Close.*

"I like your attitude. What is your manager's name?" he asked.

"Drake Fletcher is the one here now."

"Now? You mean he's leaving?" Gareth asked.

She nodded. "He owns New Hope with others. Alex Henderson and his wife, Ziva, live here in Tabiq. When they visit the States, Mr. Fletcher fills in. So don't worry, we are always well-supervised." Brooke had to admit, Alex was more easygoing than Drake. It was no surprise as Alex was an author, and he looked at everything like it was going to be in his next book. *I'm sure a clumsy waitress wasn't what he was looking for.*

Gareth said, "I probably should let you get back to work and go to my room."

"There is a clam bake on the beach tonight. Maybe you and whoever you're traveling with could attend."

He replied, "I'm here alone."

*Nice.* She needed to remind herself he was a guest and she was not to fraternize with them. *No matter how tempting they were.* But she wasn't flirting. Brooke was only providing him with valuable information. If she learned that he was there by himself, it was because he chose to share it.

"There are many people, not just couples, attending. It's a great way to start your vacation."

"You know this from experience?" he asked.

"No. I haven't personally been, but I hear the other guests raving about it."

"Then I'd very much like it if you join me."

Her eyes widened and her heart raced. What was she supposed to say? She knew she wanted to jump at the offer, but what if Drake found out? There was no way he wouldn't. The staff would surely see her, and it would be talked about and then she'd be . . . *fired.*

"Although that's a very sweet offer, I cannot accept it."

"Don't like clams?" Gareth asked. "Or maybe it's me."

She smirked. "Both appealing, but there is a company policy about not . . . getting personal with any guest." She thought that had been very tactfully said. *Mom would be*

8

*impressed.* Her mother had driven manners into her along with the art of saying no in a polite way.

"Damn. We have the same policy where I work. But I've learned there is always a work-around. Are there any rules against you attending the clam bake and happening to bump into me and maybe just happening to share a table?"

"No tables, but blankets. And I don't believe there are any rules against that."

Gareth smiled. "Great. Then it's *not* a date. And I hope to see you there tonight. I'll be sure to bring a blanket big enough for two. Enjoy your afternoon, Brooke."

Her mouth gaped open as Gareth left before she could decline. It was a brief encounter, but she learned a lot about him. Whoever Gareth, she knew he wasn't a rule follower, and he was used to getting what he wanted. He might be very easy on the eyes, but that man was . . . dangerous. Maybe not in a violent way, but in the way her mother warned her about. *A heartbreaker.*

Janet, her immediate supervisor approached. "Hi, Brooke. I really hate to ask, but we're short-staffed tonight. Would you be willing to pull a double? I'll make sure you are very well compensated."

And there was her out without having to explain why she stood Gareth up. Smiling, she said, "You know me, always happy to help."

She could feel Janet eying her. "A little mishap?"

"You could say that. I believe we might have a guest who is less than pleased with me right now."

Janet laughed. "I can almost guess which one too. Drake asked me to keep my eye on him."

"High maintenance?" Brooke asked.

"Not really sure. Drake was vague. That's not unusual for him though. You know the saying."

"You know what you need to know. I heard the speech." For the most part, it worked for her. It kept her out of any drama.

Janet snickered. "It's funny, because people from Tabiq don't want to know anything. They don't ask questions either. They come, do their job, and go home. I'm not sure I'll ever get used to that."

"Me neither. But you have to admit, they are hard workers, and I doubt they ever dumped a frozen drink on a guest," Brooke admitted.

"That's because they keep their distance. I understand why, but New Hope has been open for a few years now; you would think they'd have loosened up," Janet said. "Guess it's going to take a lot more than a job to get them to come around."

"Is it a cultural thing?" Brooke asked.

Janet shrugged. "It's funny. I can tell there's something holding them back, but I can't put my finger on it. When I ask someone, it's like a wall goes up and that person usually quits. Now I just manage and have stopped asking. Really, as long as New Hope is successful and the guests are happy, my job is done. Speaking of that, we both better get back to ours. It's going to be a busy night. Thanks again for filling in. I owe you, Brooke."

"No problem." Brooke bent over and finished cleaning up the last remnants of the drink that remained on the floor. Janet was right about one thing, it was going to be a long night, because it'd already been a long day. *But at least I won't be anywhere near the beach.* She never thought that would be something she was looking forward to.

# 2

"Damn it, Gareth. My wedding is in a few weeks. You couldn't wait until after that to take off?" Dylan questioned.

"Hey, you know me. I can't sit in the office that long. Besides, all that talk about weddings and babies was driving me nuts. At this rate, you guys will be lucky if I come back to work at all." There was part of him that wasn't joking. He never wanted to work for Lawson Steel. Not in the aspect he was. He enjoyed meeting with customers and doing background research, but the day-to-day routine bored the hell out of him.

"Charles is pissed that you disappeared too. We were counting on you to pick up the slack."

"Dylan, what slack is there? Seth practically lives in the office and looks like he's in heaven. Jordan and Ethan are backing you and Charles. What exactly is it that should hold me there?" The silence confirmed it. He wasn't really needed.

"Gareth, I get it more than any of the others. We're the jeans and T-shirt guys. But Lawson Steel belongs to all six of us. No one wants to step on your toes and make decisions for you."

"And you don't have to. I'll be back. What really can happen in a few weeks?"

"My wedding," Dylan reminded him.

Gareth laughed. "Oh yeah. That. Since I'm your best man, you should know I'll be back in time."

"And because you're my best man, I'd have thought you'd be here."

*Fuck.* He could hear the disappointment in Dylan's voice. His brother needed him there. Gareth wanted to explain to him he wasn't just fucking around. What better wedding gift could he give Dylan than securing the family's good name stayed just that?

Dylan added, "I really hope she's worth it, Gareth, because Sofia is going to be livid if you're not here."

Translated to, *I won't forgive you, Gareth, so don't fuck up.* "You can tell that beautiful bride-to-be that I will be home not only for the wedding, but also to throw your ass one hell of a bachelor party."

"At least I know you wouldn't miss that. Keep in touch though. Too many changes lately, and it's left me feeling . . . uneasy."

"Is something going on that I don't know about?" Gareth assumed he was the only one keeping secrets. That was a foolish assumption.

"Brice called me last night."

"What did he want?" Gareth asked.

"That's what was odd. I don't think he wanted anything. Just called to say hello."

Gareth wasn't buying that. "That's good, I guess."

"Nothing is ever that simple, Gareth, and you know it. If a Henderson calls, they want something. Guess time will reveal what that is."

*Yeah, they want to keep a close eye on us.* That only

confirmed Gareth's initial thoughts. Brice wasn't keeping his family abreast of any new developments. *Because he doesn't know what shit we're hiding.* It was so tempting to come clean with Brice and lay all the cards on the table. But he didn't trust Brice to be totally honest. And why should Brice be? He had nothing to gain by divulging their secrets and everything to lose.

He didn't want Dylan worrying or even thinking about the Hendersons right now. "Who knows or cares what Brice's motive was for calling? Your name has been on the news lately with your upcoming nuptials. He might have been looking for an invite. You didn't extend one, did you?"

"Hell no. If I had my way, I'd elope. You would not believe what Sofia's parents are planning. And with Sofia being pregnant, she is too . . . emotional for me to talk to her about it."

Gareth laughed. "Is it too early for me to say I told you so? If you're not careful, you'll be buying a house with a white picket fence and getting a puppy."

"Glad you think this is funny, Gareth. Better watch yourself or you might come back from your trip hitched yourself," Dylan joked.

"There's not enough booze in the world for that to happen." Gareth could hear Sofia calling out for Dylan. "Guess that is your cue to hang up. See you in a few weeks."

"Make it two. I'll talk to you later. She wants to go out for ice cream." In barely a whisper, Dylan added, "Our freezer is full of it, but somehow none of it is the kind she's craving. How the hell did Dad do this six times?"

Laughing, Gareth said, "Now you know why he worked so much. I suggest you find that flavor fast or it won't matter when I return."

Gareth ended the call and silently wished his brother luck.

13

Sofia wasn't close to her delivery date, and he wasn't sure how Dylan was going to survive this. The last time he saw Dylan, he looked like he'd been out partying for days. *And everyone says settling down is good for you. It looks like it's gonna kill him instead.* Yet another reason to remain single as far as he was concerned.

Since he was single, there was nothing holding him back from enjoying the company of that beauty, Brooke. And if he was lucky, he might be able to obtain some information from her as well. After all, she worked for them. Even if she didn't have any dirty little secrets about them, she would have a personal opinion of who she thought they were.

Gareth needed someone who wasn't so close to the situation to provide him that information. He'd hoped Roy would've been able to do that, but fear was a powerful tool, and Roy, for some reason, was afraid.

There was no way it was only from what was in the file. Someone had to have reached out to Roy and scared him off. But who, and what did they say? What Gareth didn't understand was why Roy wouldn't admit it. The Lawsons weren't pushovers and had no issue with standing up to the Hendersons. If they had threatened Roy, Gareth could've protected him. But would Brice go to those lengths in order to keep the truth hidden? *Guess it depends on what the truth is.*

Gareth hoped that coming to Tabiq was going to give him some insight to what that might be. Although the staff seemed to be friendly, they were all business. No one hung around for small talk. Normally that would be a good thing, but it limited Gareth with asking them questions, at least not ones directly related to New Hope. It wasn't like he thought the answers would just drop into his lap, but being here only made him question things more.

*Why build here?*

This was a five-star all-inclusive resort that would appeal to anyone, but in a country that didn't have enough money to subsidize itself. The road from the airport to the resort highlighted a vast difference in class. He couldn't close his eyes and ignore it. Rundown homes in the distance and vehicles on the road that looked like they should be in a junkyard. Were the Hendersons so greedy as to prey upon the less fortunate? He couldn't see any other reason for them building here. He hoped he was wrong, because the last thing he wanted was more reasons not to want the Henderson family to be his relatives.

The only personal contact he'd ever had with them was with Brice a few weeks ago. But if Brooke was right, he was about to get the opportunity to meet another one very soon. Alex was probably going to be the easiest for Gareth to deal with as he seemed much more laid-back than his brothers. And if Brice kept to his word and didn't share any information, Alex wouldn't have any clue as to their relations. *So there won't be any reason to lie to my face.*

This might be the break he was hoping for. Gareth was going to need to use Lawson Steel as the reason behind this trip. The perfect cover. And since Gareth wasn't on the sales side like Jordan and Ethan, there was no risk that Alex would consider hiring them. Gareth never thought he'd see the day he intentionally fucked up, but there's a first for everything.

With Alex arriving tomorrow, it gave Gareth plenty of time to come up with some half-assed sales pitch. He'd make the pricing so high it'd almost look like a joke, but close enough that Alex wouldn't suspect anything. That would leave most of the evening free for . . . more enjoyable things.

He needed to eat, and since he invited Brooke to join him, he should at least show up. Whether or not she would remain to be seen. She appeared to be the total opposite of him. A rule follower. If she thought the company wouldn't approve, she wouldn't do it. That was disappointing, because she was a very attractive woman and would've provided a sweet distraction for tonight.

The way things were going, Brooke probably wouldn't want to upset a guest, so she'd show up, and then she'd be reprimanded. Jobs like this didn't appear easy to come by in Tabiq, so ensuring she didn't lose it would be the nice thing to do.

He picked up the phone in his room and dialed the front desk to leave her a message. Gareth hung up the phone before they answered. Her shift would've been over long ago. *Looks like I'm going to a clam bake.*

Gareth was overdressed for such an occasion, and quickly changed into a pair of khaki shorts and a T-shirt. He slipped his cell phone into his back pocket and headed for the beach. The time difference meant no one should be calling. They didn't expect him to answer when he was . . . vacationing. Which made him question why the hell Dylan really called. There was no way Dylan believed Gareth would miss his wedding. And Dylan knew for a fact Gareth wanted nothing to do with the planning of it either. Was his brother getting cold feet? It was a huge leap from playboy to husband and dad.

*Fuck.* Gareth had been so focused on finding answers in Tabiq, he never thought his brother might actually have needed him there. He knew Dylan could handle anything that came along on the business side. However, with all the personal changes happening in his life, he might be freaking out.

Gareth normally would be more than happy to give advice and guidance. But what did he know about any of this shit other than if it was him, he'd have run for the hills?

Tomorrow Gareth would have to suck it up and call Charles. He'd get the normal lecture for being irresponsible and leaving Lawson Steel in a lurch, which wasn't the case at all. But it would be worth it if he at least gave Charles the heads-up to hang close to Dylan. The last thing he wanted was his kid brother to unravel while he was here in Tabiq.

"Excuse me. Mr. . . . Gareth, do you have a minute?"

He knew whose sweet voice was calling him. He turned, surprised to see her still dressed in her uniform "Not quite beach attire."

"I'm really sorry. I was asked to work a double. Unfortunately I won't be able to . . . bump into you at the clam bake. But I'm glad to see you're still going. They even have someone singing and playing an acoustic guitar tonight. You should have a lovely time."

Gareth wasn't really a sit-back, do-nothing guy. His idea of being on the beach at night would entail taking in the sight of the moon with some sexy woman and a bottle of wine, clothes optional. Lying on a blanket, alone, listening to music sounded boring as hell.

"It's unfortunate you're going to miss it. Do they do this to you often?" he asked.

She shook her head. "I've been here for a few years, and it's happened only a few times. Janet, my supervisor, would've picked up the shift if I didn't want it. Really, this is an amazing place to work. Most places only worry about the guests being happy, but here they take into consideration the staff's needs as well."

"That is nice to hear." *And surprising since I know who you work for.* "Maybe you can *bump* into me another time. What's on the schedule for tomorrow night?"

Brooke laughed. "Karaoke. But you don't want to hear me sing. I sound like a cat when you step on its tail."

"That's hard to believe. Your voice is—"

"Trust me. And no, I'm not about to prove I'm telling you the truth either. I don't even sing in the shower; it's that bad."

Gareth laughed. "Wow, it really must be horrific." He played along, but didn't buy it for an instant. It was more likely that she was shy.

"Let me guess, you're a performer and are dying to sing."

"Not even close. I'm in the steel business, and I've never sung karaoke either. But a place like this must have other things happening." *Like a real night life.*

"There are, but most people come here to spend their time on the beach or in the saltwater pools, which are amazing as well. What do you like to do on vacation?" she asked.

*Drink. Party. Sleep late.* That wasn't much different than his normal routine, just the location changed. It wasn't as though he wasn't a responsible person. He took business seriously, but when he wasn't working, he liked to play and play hard. What was wrong with that? *The life of a bachelor. Perfect.* "A variety of things. Maybe we can discuss it over dinner tomorrow?"

Brooke smirked. "I think we discussed this before. I can't—"

"Eat? Because I'm sure there aren't laws against that, even in Tabiq," he teased.

"Are you going to ask me each time we run into each other?" she inquired.

"You do want me to enjoy my stay here, don't you?"

"Trust me, my company isn't all that exciting."

*So you want me to believe.* "Why don't you let me be the judge of that?"

"But I explained our policy," she stated.

That was very easy to resolve. "Then have dinner with me off the resort."

Her eyes widened, and she said, "Guests are strongly encouraged to stay on the premises."

"This isn't a prison." Her comment, however, made him want to know more. "Unless there is a valid reason to tell me where I can and can't go."

Brooke looked serious for a moment and said, "It's not something we talk about. But for your own safety, it is highly recommended you do not leave the resort, at least not alone."

If it was dangerous, he wasn't about to encourage her to accompany him. "Then if you don't want me to wander off on my own, I suggest you have dinner with me tomorrow here on the resort." She had walked right into that, and he was confident he was coming out the victor. *I always do.*

"I guess you have left me no choice. Dinner it is. How about I meet you at five? That way if you change your mind, you can still go out and enjoy the karaoke."

"More likely a walk on the beach. I better let you get back to work, before you accuse me of trying to get you fired."

"Is that your plan?" she asked.

He shook his head. "No ulterior motive here. Just dinner."

She peered at him before saying, "Then I guess I'll see you at five. Have a good night."

Normally women hung all over him. She definitely wasn't his type, a live-for-the-moment kind of girl. At least that is the feel he got in their few short encounters. He normally was spot on when it came to that sort of stuff. Yet here he was, chasing after the one who had shot him down twice. He might be bored, but boredom wasn't what had him watching the sway of her hips as she walked away. He found several things about her very . . . enticing. But damn, there was no way she didn't know he was checking her out. She could play hard to get all she wanted, but he saw right through that act. She was interested, but it wasn't just her job holding her back. Maybe tomorrow he'd find out what it was.

*Not that I should care. I'm not going to be here long anyway.*

Brooke turned the corner and only then let out a long exhale. What was it with him? He was supposed to be here on vacation, yet he didn't seem like he wanted to do anything . . . fun. She shouldn't judge, but someone who looked like him and seemed so . . . confident, shouldn't have an issue with going out and mingling with new people. Yet the only one he seemed interested in speaking to was her.

*Who would come all the way to Tabiq just to talk to me? Hell, I wouldn't even do that.* She snickered to herself. If she had her way, she'd be doing everything the resort had to offer. Although she didn't let it show, she was much more adventurous than any of her friends. They were all "responsible" as they always reminded her. At times the little digs irritated her, but for the most part, she felt bad for them. They all were back home doing and being what their parents expected of them. Brooke was far from being a follower. And her parents loved and accepted her for who she was. A free spirit who wasn't afraid to take chances and try new experiences. The fact that she opted to spend a year working in a resort at a remote location said it all.

Maybe if she spent some time with Gareth, she'd rub off on him. Not to the point of singing karaoke, but doing something fun would be better than nothing. Once he was out there and talking to others, he'd quickly forget she was there, unless he needed to order food.

That really wasn't very flattering, but it was the truth. Her gift of gab came in handy as a waitress. People were drawn to her to chat. That's all this was with Gareth. One dinner with him and he'd relax. Although he joked with her, she could still tell he was uptight about something. He wasn't the first man who'd come to New Hope and struggled. There were some who'd come to escape personal problems. That never worked. Problems followed you no matter where you went. Others were work-alcoholics and they were the worst. They felt guilty about having fun, so they chose not to.

Was that his issue? Was his job overwhelming and burning him out? Could he bring himself to stop thinking about business long enough to play a little? No. It couldn't be that, because he was willing to take a break to have dinner with her. So if you scratch off personal problems and business, what was left?

*Hell if I know. I'm not a psychologist.*

No matter what brought Gareth there, New Hope was probably just what he needed. How was she going to get him to see that without getting herself fired? If she was smart, she'd just walk away and let Gareth do what he wanted. But for some crazy-ass reason, she couldn't do that. She also couldn't bring herself to approach the activity leaders and asked them do their job and coax him into things.

Brooke knew what she needed to do. She looked at her watch and hesitated to call so late, but not only did she need Janet's approval, she needed to cover her ass. Looking around to confirm no one was in earshot, she dialed Janet's number.

"Hello, Brooke. Is everything okay? Wait. That was a stupid question. Of course there's a problem. You never call me after hours. Do you need me to return to the resort?" Janet asked quickly.

"Oh God, no. I wasn't even sure if I should call you this late."

"Brooke, it's only ten. That's not late. And besides, I

know you wouldn't call unless it was important. So why don't you tell me what's going on."

"There's this man. I don't know what to do."

"Is he harassing you? You know we don't tolerate that. I can have him removed immediately if—"

"That's not it. He just seems . . . lost. I'm not sure if that's the right way to explain it. He says he's a guest, but he doesn't seem interested in doing anything." *Except having dinner with me.*

"Maybe he just wants to enjoy some quiet time on the beach. Many people just come to soak up the sun."

That would be a logical thought, but she knew there was something more. Gareth was a mystery, and one she wanted to solve. This was crazy. Why was she giving him a second thought? She should've declined his offer and kept moving. But no, she stood talking with him because . . . she wanted to. Whatever lame excuse she was giving Janet for having dinner with him was just that, an excuse. Yet that didn't seem to stop her from making them. "I know, but I don't think he's made it down there. Each time I suggest one of our activities, he asks me to join him."

"Like a date?" Janet inquired.

*I wish.* "No. I don't think so." This guy probably had woman dying to go out with him. No way would he ask a waitress out. "Maybe he just doesn't know how to have . . . fun." That was hard for her to believe. Gareth didn't look like a sheltered man in the least.

"And what did you say when he asked?"

*Where have you been all my life?* She wasn't one to fall all over a guy, but Gareth was a very handsome man. He also made her laugh, a trait she loved. She didn't say no, because she couldn't bring herself to.

But not telling Janet she found him attractive wasn't actually lying, was it? Since Janet didn't ask that question directly, she would answer only what she'd asked. "The first two times I declined his offer. But he asked if I would join him for dinner tomorrow night. I ran out of ways to say no, so I agreed to meet him at five. But I wanted your approval before actually moving forward with this."

"Date?"

"No. I asked him what he liked to do for fun, and he said we could discuss it over dinner. It would be unfortunate if he traveled all this way just to spend his entire vacation sitting in his room. Maybe if I can talk to him a bit longer, he will see how much New Hope really has to offer."

"And you don't think one of our activity leaders could do the same? I mean that is what they are paid for."

*And I'm paid to be a waitress. I know.* Normally she loved her job. It's just this once, she wanted . . . more. "I can't explain it, but he seems . . . comfortable talking to me. If you'd rather I let him know I can't make it, I'll do so." But she really was looking forward to hearing what Gareth liked doing during his free time. He'd piqued her interest, and not on a professional level either. There was more to him than he let on. And she wanted to know what it was.

"Okay. Have dinner with him. But if you find he's not . . . the introvert you believe him to be, back off. I don't want to see you being . . . manipulated in any way. Tabiq has a reputation for some disturbing things, and New Hope won't stand for *any* of it."

Brooke was glad to hear that, but it opened up the question as to why New Hope was so firm on this policy. Had they encountered a problem before? She knew the locals definitely kept their distance from any outsiders. Even though she worked with them, it wasn't like anyone ever invited her to their home for dinner. Actually, she didn't know much about any of them at all. If it weren't for Janet and a few others, Brooke might not have stayed. No matter how beautiful the resort was, she needed adult interaction and conversation to survive.

"Okay Janet. I promise, if things don't feel right, I'll let you know." *And if it feels too good, I'll keep it to myself.*

"Thanks for calling me, Brooke. By the way, what is the name of this guest?"

"Gareth." Funny, she didn't even know his last name. But Janet had access to room records and how many Gareths could there be staying at the resort this week?

"I don't think I've crossed paths with him yet either. Keep me posted."

"Will do. Good night," Brooke said and ended the call.

She slipped her phone back in the pocket of her black apron. That call went better than she'd expected. In a way, she just got Janet's blessing to have dinner with Gareth. With any luck, that dinner would turn into something fun on the beach. *He's going to enjoy this vacation even if I have to make him.*

As she made her way back toward the kitchen, she chuckled to herself. *And I'm finally going to get to have some fun too.*

---

## 3

"Charles, staying there wasn't going to change anything. What Dylan needs isn't my advice, it's yours. Be glad I'm not giving him a sympathy card instead of a wedding card."

"You're lucky Rosslyn isn't here listening to you right now," Charles warned.

*Exactly my point.* Gareth didn't dance around watching his words. Rosslyn seemed to have already figured that out. "She's not that delicate wallflower you make her out to be. Hell, she's running Grayson Corp. From what Dylan told me, she's not a pushover either. Thankfully, she's not her uncle Maxwell, or we might all be in trouble."

"Just because she's strong, doesn't mean she'd appreciate your comments. And for the record, I wasn't protecting her; I was protecting your dumb ass."

"Ouch. Where are your HR words?" Gareth asked teasingly.

Charles laughed. "Probably out on vacation just like you. Good thing the others are picking up all the slack."

"What slack are you guys talking about? From what I saw before I left, we had nothing pending. The only thing I'm missing is baby and wedding talk. You can have both of those." Gareth wasn't ignorant enough to think the day-to-day work wouldn't back up a bit, but it was nothing he couldn't handle when he returned. If something was pressing, his brothers would handle it. *They always do.*

"That is beside the point. You can't just take off anytime you want."

"What's the point of owning a company if you need to ask permission?" Gareth asked sarcastically.

"And what's the point of owning a company if you're not going to be here to run it? Where exactly are you, by the way?" Charles asked.

*Fuck.* He'd been hoping to avoid that question. "A tropical island soaking up the sun."

"What you mean is that it's none of my business," Charles stated.

"Did you really want to hear all about it?" Gareth asked.

"No. You can keep all those details to yourself. Should we expect you back next week?"

"I don't have a return date yet, but I promised Dylan I would be back in plenty of time to throw him a bachelor party."

Charles sighed. "Do you really think that is necessary?"

"Just because you didn't want one, doesn't mean he doesn't," Gareth clarified. "Don't worry, Charles. I'm not ordering strippers. I was actually thinking we'd fly out to Vegas for the night and try our luck."

"You don't think we are lucky enough?" Charles asked.

"Are you becoming Dad? Old and no fun?"

"I'm nothing like Dad. And if you even say Granddad, I'll come find you and kick your ass. The last thing I want is to be anything like our ancestors."

He could hear the anger in Charles's voice. "What's got

26

you so pissed off?" Charles didn't answer so Gareth added, "Listen, I know I joke around a lot, but if there is something you want to talk about, I'm here."

"Dad made a comment yesterday when he was holding Penelope."

"What did he say?" Their father was unpredictable so Gareth didn't even want to take a guess.

"He said he hoped she didn't grow up to be like her auntie."

"And you think he meant Aunt Audrey?" Gareth asked.

"Who else would he mean? She was the only female on either side, and since Dylan isn't married yet, I doubt he was talking about Sofia."

That was a fucked-up statement. But what shocked him more was his father making it. "I thought he didn't know anything. This sounds like he was—"

"Lying. I know. What I don't get is why would he lie to us? Dylan said he spoke to him. That was Dad's time to come clean with everything he knew. He should know us by now. If we want to know something, we won't stop until we get it."

*Ain't that the truth?* "Maybe he thought he was protecting us."

"I think he's protecting himself. There's something going on, Gareth, and I can't figure it out. When you come back, I think we should continue looking into the connection between us and the Hendersons."

Now Gareth felt like an asshole. Obviously Charles didn't know he and Dylan already met with Brice. The timing wasn't good to bring that up now. It was going to cause problems, and Gareth wasn't there to intervene.

"I think you're right. But can't this wait a few weeks? Let Dylan and Sofia have their wedding, and then you and I can sit down and talk about everything we know and plan out what to do about the missing pieces." This should buy him some time. Gareth doubted he'd know it all, but anything he could learn was less to worry about later.

"Okay. We'll table it for now. But I have to tell you, Dad's slipping and I don't want him saying something that will cause a scandal for the family," Charles said. "We need to know so we can prepare for damage control."

"Got it. I'll try to cut this trip short. But my dinner date is about here, and I don't want to keep her waiting." Gareth hadn't left his room yet, but he would soon, and that was the fastest excuse he could come up with.

"Someday, Gareth, you'll settle down."

Gareth laughed. "And look whose mind is slipping now," he teased. "I'll text you when I'm on my way back to the States."

As soon as he ended the call, he dialed Dylan's number.

"Are you calling to let me know you're coming back?" Dylan asked.

"Ha. If you saw the beautiful woman I'm having dinner with, you wouldn't rush me." Brooke definitely was stunning, but that wasn't what he wanted to talk about. "I only have a few minutes, but I wanted to let you know, I just got off the phone with Charles."

"Let me guess. He's pissed that you're gone."

"That too. But he was more upset with Dad. He wants me to start looking into the Henderson connection after the wedding. You can't let him know we already met with Brice. If he finds out, he's going to want to know everything."

"And that's a bad thing why?" Dylan asked.

"Because your bride-to-be will not get the wedding she wants. Instead she'll be caught in the middle of family drama. I don't know much about shit like this, but I don't think that's going to be good for her, the baby, or you."

"Gareth, I've got to be honest, there are times I wish we hadn't met with Brice. Some of the things he said haunt me. This is our gene pool we're talking about. I don't think it worried me until I learned I was going to be a father. Now . . . it makes me sick. They are not the stories I want to tell my child."

"And you won't have to. Trust me Dylan; no one wants the truth to come out. That's why you can't say anything to Charles. Just let it lie for now."

"I thought that was our plan. You make it seem like something has changed. What aren't you telling me, Gareth? And don't give me a bullshit line about some woman. Where are you?" Dylan demanded.

"Tabiq."

"What the hell are you doing there?" Dylan snapped.

"Gee. Would you believe I'm on vacation?" Gareth asked sarcastically. "Didn't think so. I'm trying to find out why the Hendersons are here. You do know they have built a multi-billion dollar resort here, don't you?"

"Charles mentioned something about Brice wanting a contract with the Lawsons. Was that it?"

"No. This is different. From what I can tell, it's only a few years old. But why here? It doesn't fit. This country is . . . poor. And I'm not sure about the crime rate, but they don't want any guests leaving the resort alone."

"That isn't the only place that has those types of recommendations. You've traveled enough to know that," Dylan added. "But you could've done all that research from New York. Why go there?"

"Do you remember Brice stating they were making amends for what his father had done?"

"I do. And I remember him saying that Great-granddad was connected as well."

He was trying to forget that part. "Well, we're not going to find that information on the internet. So I came here to learn firsthand."

Dylan laughed. "You went halfway around the world to see if some stranger would tell you the Hendersons' dirty little secrets? You should've told me, Gareth. I would've let you know you're wasting your time."

"You have a better idea?"

"Yes."

"Let's hear it," Gareth said.

"Let's sit down with Brice again, and this time we demand he tell us everything."

Gareth laughed. "And you really think that will work? Because if someone demanded we do something we didn't want to do, I don't think they'd be leaving happy at all."

"You're right. I'm just . . . unsure what to do. And I definitely don't like the idea of you in Tabiq by yourself. If Brice finds out you're probing for info, there is going to be hell to pay. I can't have your back from where I am."

"And I don't need you to. Trust me. I'm not going to stir the pot. Just here on vacation, that's all. Oh. I'm meeting with Alex Henderson too."

"What the hell for?" Dylan snapped.

"To sell him steel of course."

"You want to do business with them now?" Dylan asked.

"Nope. But I'm going to make it look like I do. Hence why I'm here in Tabiq. Just a sales call, that's all."

"You're fucking nuts if you think they are going to believe that."

"Dylan, Alex doesn't know about us. He's just going to look at me and tell me no. That simple. No worries."

"Great. You're in a foreign country taking on a family

that doesn't want to know us. At least if you don't make it back, I'll know where to start looking."

"We're not dealing with murderers here."

"And you know that how?" Dylan asked. "Exactly. You're there because we don't know what we're dealing with. Every time we think it is bad, it seems to get worse."

"And that is why we need to know. I don't give a shit what James Henderson did. But if a Lawson was connected, and I don't just mean Aunt Audrey, then we need to know."

"You don't have to worry, I'm not telling Charles anything about this. If he knew what you were doing, he'd be on a flight there to confront your ass."

"I don't answer to him, Dylan." *I don't answer to anyone.*

"Try telling him that. Hey, Sofia is calling me. I've got to go. You better check in with me every day or I *will* tell him. Got it?"

"Sure. Daily updates. Got it." Gareth ended the call. Dylan was at the breaking point, and this was just another weight on his shoulders. He wasn't sure calling him was the right thing to do, but it was too late now.

He slipped his phone in his pocket and made his way downstairs. When he arrived at the lobby he asked the front desk if Alex Henderson had arrived yet.

"He has. Is there something I can assist you with?"

"I was hoping to meet with him."

"Do you have an appointment?" she asked.

*Do I need one?* "No. Why don't you just call him and let him know Gareth Lawson from Lawson Steel is here."

She looked at him for a moment, picked up the phone, and made the call. She whispered so low he couldn't hear her. When she hung the receiver up she turned back to Gareth and said, "He'll be right up. If you'd like to take a seat, it'll be a few minutes."

31

"Thank you." He walked over to stand by the large stone fireplace, one he couldn't picture ever being lit. The climate here was different levels of hot. At least it was a dry heat, unlike a tropical island where the humidity was unbearable. Overall, he had to admit, the Hendersons had pulled off one hell of a resort. They used natural resources to generate the electricity and, from what he'd seen so far, most of their food was grown or raised here as well. There wasn't much New Hope needed the outside world for. He didn't believe that was an accident. But why create a place for people to come if they didn't want them here? He was missing something. As Alex entered the lobby, it seemed as though he was about to find out.

"Hello. I'm Alex Henderson. You wanted to speak to me?"

Gareth extended his hand. "I'm Gareth Lawson with Lawson Steel. I'm currently a guest here, but I was hoping you had time to discuss a bit of business."

"I don't believe you're one of our contractors," Alex stated.

"No we are not." *And I don't think we ever will be.*

"I'm not the person you want to speak to regarding contracts. You might want to call our Boston office and ask to speak to Dean or Shaun. Either of them could assist you. I hope you didn't travel all this way just to meet with me."

Gareth shook his head. "No. I wanted to get a look at the facility firsthand. It's quite . . . impressive. It's a hidden gem that many people don't know about. With the right marketing, this place could easily expand."

"We're pretty set with things as they are at New Hope."

"Really? I'd think your family would be looking at the developmental potential. When I flew in, I noticed there is another side to the island that doesn't looked touched. If the

Hendersons aren't building there, I might know some investors who would be very interested."

"And they would find they are not welcome."

"Do you speak for the entire country?" Gareth asked. He knew it sounded rude, but he wasn't opposed to pushing buttons to get what he wanted.

Alex glared at him and said firmly, "We are very protective of what happens in Tabiq."

"And why is that?" Gareth asked.

Alex cocked a brow. "Why do I have a feeling you're not here to sell steel?"

"What other reason would I have?"

"This isn't a conversation I'd like to have in the lobby. What do you say we discuss it over dinner?" Alex suggested.

Gareth had plans with Brooke, but no matter how much he was looking forward to them, he'd break their date. He didn't think he was going to get a second shot at this. "Sounds good. Where should we meet?"

"Not here. My home is close by. I'll let Ziva know we're having company. That is if you don't mind leaving the resort for a few hours."

*Hell no.* "I look forward to it. What time should I be ready?"

"I like to eat with my family, so I'd say we leave at six, if that is convenient."

"It is."

"Gareth, this is *my* family home you're being invited to. I won't tolerate any disrespect," Alex warned.

"Understood." Although he was thrilled for the invitation, he also was a bit surprised. It definitely couldn't be something Alex did on a regular basis. It was going to be an enlightening evening. *Hell, Brice couldn't wait to get rid of us.*

33

Before Gareth went to his room he went back to the desk. "Would you have an envelope and paper?"

"Of course." She handed him the items and he picked up a pen from the desk.

BROOKE. WILL NEED TO RESCHEDULE DINNER. HOPE YOU'RE FREE TOMORROW NIGHT. SAME TIME. GARETH

He inserted the noted, sealed the envelope, then handed it back to the woman. "Could you please ensure Brooke receives this sometime today? Actually, the earlier the better."

"Certainly. If I'm correct, she is working in the main dining room today if you'd prefer to give it to her directly."

"I'd rather not," Gareth replied.

She nodded and said, "I'll have someone take it to her right away. Will there be anything else, Mr. Lawson?"

"No. That's it. Thank you." He felt like an ass not reaching out to her in person, but she was a distraction. Even the way she looked at him was enough to make him lose sight of what he was doing in Tabiq. He couldn't afford to lose focus tonight. It was going to be hard enough for him to hold back and not ask a million questions that were running through his mind. If it was just Alex, fuck it, he'd let loose. But it wasn't only his home he was going to, they had a little girl too. Brice would fuck anyone up for upsetting his little niece. He definitely wasn't going to say or do anything to upset Alex's daughter.

The afternoon flew. Gareth spent most of it researching Alex and found he was nothing like his brothers. *A murder mystery author. Not the tycoon the others are.* It also might explain why Alex invited him tonight. *Might be using me for the next book.*

But as he and Alex pulled up to the house and got out of

the car, Gareth had second thoughts about going inside. Charisa, Alex's daughter, came running out and Ziva was right behind her, catching her by the hand.

"No running," Ziva said firmly.

"But Mommy, Daddy is home," Charisa cried out, tugging Ziva.

Ziva didn't let go and said, "I see that. And Daddy has brought home a guest. Remember what I said?"

The girl nodded, her dark ponytail bouncing in the air. "To listen and not get all excited. But Daddy is home. He's been gone all day."

Alex turned to Gareth and said, "Like I said, this is my family."

"I hope I'm not intruding," he replied.

Alex opened his arms wide and Ziva let Charisa's hand go. She rushed over to Alex, and he scooped her up, tossing her high into the air before catching her.

"Alex, that is *not* helping," Ziva snapped.

Charisa laughed. "Again Daddy. Again."

After a few more times Alex said, "Okay, pumpkin. That's enough for tonight. My arms are going to get so stretched out I'll be stepping on my fingers when I walk."

She hugged her dad and said, "I'll help you so you don't." Then she looked at Gareth and said, "Maybe he can help too."

Gareth smiled at her. "I think you're all your daddy needs."

Alex said, "Come on inside. I'm sure Ziva has something delicious planned for us." Before they entered, he did the introductions. "You met my little pumpkin. Her name is Charisa. And this lovely lady is Ziva, my wife."

"A pleasure to meet you," Gareth said.

"And the high-pitched scream you are hearing is our son, Nikko," Alex added.

"That's my cue. Nice to meet you too, but it seems all this noise has woken the baby. Alex can show you around, and I'll join you all in a few minutes."

When Ziva was gone, Alex added, "She's amazing at everything she does, but when I watch her with the kids, I'm blown away. She has the patience of a saint." He laughed. "Then again, she has to. She married me."

He was tempted to say he agreed, but tonight he'd play nice. This was about getting to know his cousin in a different way. Not business. Not the past either. Just the family man standing before him.

Dinner was pretty much what he would expect at any normal household. Charisa talked about what she and Ziva had done all day. Which included being shown a slew of finger painted pictures and one that looked like she was trying to write her name.

"I think you have your daddy's artistic genes," Gareth said.

Charisa made a face. "I don't like jeans. I like dresses."

Gareth laughed. "And you look very pretty in them. I have a niece and her mommy puts her in dresses too."

"Can she come over and play?" Charisa asked.

"She lives in New York," Gareth replied.

"Charisa, you know your cousins live in Boston. New York is a few hours away from there."

Charisa's eyes teared up. "I want to go to Boston and play with them. Nikko is no fun. He is a baby. He can't even walk or talk or paint or anything." Then she turned to Gareth and asked, "Can I play with your niece?"

"Sorry. Penelope is only a few months older than Nikko. She can't do any of that fun stuff either."

Charisa crossed her arms and said, "No one wants to paint with me. I bet you don't want to either."

Alex interjected. "Charisa, it's too late to paint tonight. Maybe he can paint with you when he comes back."

Was Alex saying that to appease his daughter or was he really expecting to see him again? "That would be nice."

Charisa smiled. "Good. Maybe you know how to paint a unicorn. I want one with all the colors of the rainbow and his horn has to be gold. Real gold too."

"And where do you think you're going to get real gold, pumpkin?" Alex asked.

She tapped her chin with her finger in deep thought. Then gleefully she said, "At the end of the rainbow. That's where all the gold is."

"I think Mommy has been reading to you again," Alex said.

"No. I learned that at school."

Alex turned to Gareth and explained, "We have a pre-school here now. She will tell you she has no one to play with, but there are plenty of children her age she gets to play with."

"But that's only two times a week," Charisa pouted.

"Yes. And tomorrow is school. So why don't you tell Mr. Lawson thank you for coming to dinner and give Daddy a kiss."

"Okay, Mommy." She walked around the table and stuck her hand out to Gareth to shake. "Don't forget to bring your pot of gold next time."

He bit back laughter. "I'll see what I can do."

Then she hugged Alex and kissed him. "I love you, Daddy."

"I love you too, pumpkin."

Ziva scooped Nikko up in one arm and took Charisa by the hand. "Good night, gentlemen."

"Good night. Thank you again for dinner," Gareth said.

"You're welcome any time."

When they were alone Alex turned to him and said, "She means it. Our door is always open."

Gareth leaned back in his seat and said, "Thank you. But . . . why? You don't know me from a hole in the wall."

"I know enough," Alex said.

Cocked brow, Gareth asked, "Care to enlighten me?"

Alex leaned his elbows on the table. "Do you really think I'd have you in my home without knowing everything there is to know first?"

*Like why I'm here?* "And why do you care to know that?"

"For the same reason you want to know all about us, cousin." Gareth fought to keep a poker face and didn't acknowledge their relationship. Alex continued, "It's late and I have staff meetings tomorrow. But if you'd like, we can sit and talk."

"About anything specific?" Gareth asked.

"Depends on the questions you have. I can't promise I have all the answers, but I'll have some. Now if you don't mind, I'll have my driver take you back to the resort. I try to read a story to Charisa each night."

"Not one of yours I hope," Gareth teased.

"Ziva won't even read those," Alex laughed. "Let me see you out."

It wasn't long before Gareth was back at the resort, standing on his balcony. Brooke wasn't joking. He could hear the karaoke party going on from there. It was a good thing singing wasn't their day jobs, because it was comical, and a bit painful, to listen to. But he enjoyed hearing how much fun they were having.

Gareth was one of the Lawson men who went out frequently. But this was a different type of fun. It reminded him of his younger days when they would all vacation as a family. Charles, being the oldest, didn't always get to go. He was stuck working with their father. But the rest of the guys would do stupid shit and laugh until their ribs hurt. Gareth didn't want to be a kid again, but he had to admit he missed that carefree feeling. Life was so simple then. *Ignorance is bliss. But I can't forget what I know.*

That type of stress made him feel one hundred instead of thirty-three. If they weren't careful, they were going to end up just like their father. Old and beaten down by the world. *That's not going to happen. Not to me and not to any of them.*

He really hoped coming here wasn't actually doing more damage than good. At first he'd only thought about protecting the Lawsons. After dinner, knowing Alex knew, he no longer could look at the Hendersons as anything other than . . . *family.*

Gareth walked back into his room and closed the glass sliding doors to the balcony. He walked over to his laptop and turned it on. His mind was filled with questions, and he was left with only one fact. *Dinner just changed everything.*

4

---

Brooke knew it was only a matter of time before she bumped into Gareth. She couldn't believe he stood her up. It made no sense since he was the one who kept asking her. Was it some kind of game to him? If so, she was done with it. Next time he asked her, even for a glass of water, she was going to let him know where he could get it himself.

Who was she fooling? No matter what, he was a guest at the resort, and she'd never be intentionally rude. Not even to someone who deserved it. She just wished it didn't bother her. For the life of her, she couldn't understand why it did. Many men had asked her out since she started working there. Each time she turned them down. It was really that simple. So why didn't she just keep doing the same with Gareth? If she had, she wouldn't be left feeling . . . *stupid.*

Janet wasn't the last person she wanted to see, but close to it right now.

"How was dinner last night?"

She smiled and said, "Uneventful."

"Really? I looked at his photo and that was the last thing I thought you'd say. I was actually questioning my judgment letting you go to dinner with him. So he's handsome but boring?" Janet asked.

She shrugged. "I wouldn't know. He stood me up."

Janet's eyes widened. "You're joking, right?" Brooke shook her head. "That's horrible. Why would someone do that?"

"Because they're arrogant, and it was fun to see the look on my face when I said yes?" Last night was pretty much spent tossing and turning and that was the only explanation she could come up with.

Janet reached out and patted her on the arm. "I'm sorry. I guess you were looking forward to this *date*."

"It wasn't a date. It was—"

"Oh give me a break. No one has that look on their face when work cancels out on you. It's okay. I get it. He looked charming and those type of men are hard to resist."

"Funny, I don't see you having an issue," Brooke stated.

Janet laughed. "That's because I already have the sexiest, most charming, and best of all, sweetest man there ever was."

Brooke hadn't actually spoken to Janet's husband, Vinny, but she did rave about him all the time. It was nice to see someone happy and in love. "We can't all be as lucky as you are."

"Funny. I wasn't looking for love when I met Vinny. Actually I had just started this job, and I was so worried about being able to keep it."

"And he worked here?" Brooke asked.

"No, not at the same time I did. He had been hired to help build it. But once that was over, he decided he liked Tabiq and made it his home. Guess it's our home now."

"I can't believe you actually moved here permanently. Don't you miss the States?" Brooke loved being on the resort, but this wasn't long-term for her. Actually she only had about

41

two months left on this job before it was time to head back home. That was going to be bittersweet. She missed her parents and her friends, but she loved being on a new adventure. *There'll be more.*

"One thing about working for the Hendersons, you can hop a flight with them anytime. And they travel so frequently, I can see my parents every month. If I want to, that is." Janet gave Brooke a playful wink.

"I know. I miss being home, but after a week of being there, I'll be going crazy."

Janet looked at her and asked, "Have you ever considered taking on a permanent position here?"

She thought Janet was joking at first, but her expression was serious. Beautiful beaches and endless sunshine. It was heavenly, but something was missing. "I don't think it's for me. You have Vinny. I'd be . . . alone. It's not like we can go out and meet a local man, and policy has it that we can't date a guest. I'm not out to get hitched, but I don't want to be an old spinster either."

Janet laughed. "I think you have a few years before that happens," she teased.

"At least you didn't say months," Brooke chuckled.

Janet said, "I'm glad you're in a better mood. I was contemplating hunting Gareth Lawson down and giving him a piece of my mind."

"Please don't. It would only make things awkward."

"Not for me. And it shouldn't for you either. Mr. Lawson, on the other hand, should feel horrible."

"I'm sure something came up and it just slipped his mind." *That doesn't make it hurt any less.* It wasn't the fact he stood her up, but it made her feel . . . insignificant. That she wasn't worth remembering.

"I say you should take the afternoon off and do something

fun. Maybe spend some time on the beach, or go parasailing or diving or—"

"Reading a book on the beach sounds wonderful right now. But I can't leave you shorthanded."

"You're not. We actually are a bit overstaffed. And don't worry, I'm paying you for the full day. Consider this my thank you for pulling a double the other night."

"If you're sure."

"I am. Now go and don't look back. If you do, someone will ask you for something and you'll never get out of here," Janet said.

Brook smiled. "Isn't that always the way?"

She rushed off, went to the locker room, showered, and changed into a pair of shorts and a tank top. Brooke wasn't about to go swimming, and wearing her bikini in front of the guests felt kind of funny. This was perfect for the occasion. Alex had given her one of his books to read when she was first hired. Although she had intended to finish it, she couldn't. By the time she made it to her room every night, she was dead on her feet and ready to sleep. A gory murder mystery wasn't going to give her sweet dreams. But it was early afternoon. She had plenty of time to think of something more pleasant before bed.

As expected, there was plenty of room on the beach. After all, nightlife came with a price. Who wanted that big bright yellow ball in the sky threatening to make your hangover even worse? Brooke didn't need to worry about that. She not only didn't drink, she was a morning server, so she never stayed up past ten. At least not in New Hope. Who knew what her next job would require? *Hopefully, it'll allow me to sleep late.*

Brooke considered herself a morning person, but really, everyone wants to be able to sleep in once in a while. The problem with living where you work, was you always felt like you were at work, even when it was your day off. Guests seemed to recognize her, even without her waitress apron, and before she knew it, she was fetching someone tea, coffee, or something to eat. Not once had she even considered telling them she was off the clock. She was there to make their vacation one they would never forget.

From what she'd witnessed over the past ten months, the word about New Hope was growing. They had been busy before, but the clientele was changing. It was a younger crowd, enjoying all the amenities the resort had to offer. Heck, if she wasn't on staff, so would she.

Even though she'd been banking most of her check each week, it wasn't like she could afford to stay on as a guest. This place wasn't cheap. As a young girl, she'd stayed at more places like this than she could recall. It was nice having rich parents. However, even better than that was choosing to live without taking a cent from them.

Her friends all thought she was crazy, but it provided a sense of pride knowing everything she had or did was because she'd earned it. Of course there were times when she wanted to cave in and accept her parents' offer for a new car or a house, but why did she need those things? Brooke had an amazing life. Each year she worked doing something different. By the time the job started to get old and stagnant, it was time for her to move on.

What she hadn't done yet was plan out her next adventure. That was unlike her. She always had something in the works before now. Maybe she did like Tabiq more than she'd thought. It wasn't as though she was going to be stuck at home, it just meant that her layover visiting the folks might be longer than planned. *That will make them happy.*

They had been begging her to spend the holidays with

them, but as timing had it, the last few years she was off in another country. This past year in Tabiq, the year prior in Florence, and the year before that, on an Alaskan cruise line. People could mock her for choosing to be a waitress, but it meant she could find employment just about anywhere.

Time was slipping away, and she hadn't even opened the book. Thankfully Alex hadn't asked her what she thought of it. But she had her answer ready if he did. *Bone chilling.* She slipped her sunglasses on and opened the book. She was only on chapter three and still couldn't shake the visual of the horrific scene from chapter two. Brooke had no idea Alex could write so . . . scary. Out of all the Hendersons she'd met, he seemed the most laid-back and easy-going. But his book was about a serial killer that stalked his victims while on vacation.

She slammed the book shut. *Oh no. Not today.* She would be looking at every guest like they were a potential murderer. That would totally ruin this adventure, and not just for her either. She could only imagine what a guest would think as she started questioning them.

"For someone who tried talking me into coming to the beach, you don't look like you're enjoying it."

She didn't need to look up to know it was Gareth. "I *was* enjoying it." She hoped he picked up on the dig meant for him.

"Too hot? Book boring?" he asked.

"Company," she blurted. Instantly she wished she could take that back. No matter what her feelings were, hurt or not, he was a guest.

"Wow, and here I was thinking you didn't find me totally repulsive. Guess I was mistaken."

"Yes. I mean no . . . I mean . . . I don't find you repulsive.

You seem like a very nice person," she stammered as she tried to correct herself.

"But?"

"But what?" she asked.

"My company is what has ruined your time on the beach. Why?" Gareth inquired.

"I misspoke."

"And I don't believe you," he said flatly. "Was it the last minute cancelation last night?"

*Nailed it.* "You mean 'no show,' correct?"

He had a puzzled look on his face then said, "You didn't get my note." She shook her head. "Damn it. I should've tracked you down and told you myself. There was a change of plans, an opportunity I couldn't pass up."

"You don't need to explain yourself to me. It was nothing. Trust me, I ate anyway."

Gareth laughed. "I would hope so or I'd feel even worse than I do now. How can I make it up to you?"

"Like I said, there is no need," she said, adverting his gaze. He could laugh if he wanted to, but she wasn't.

"Not even over dinner tonight?" he asked.

This time she turned back to him and said, "I don't want to hear what your hobbies or likes are that much."

"Was that what we were going to discuss? I'd much rather hear all about you," Gareth stated.

"Not much to tell. I like to read. I like to sail. I like . . . just about everything. No food allergies, and I've had all my shots. There it is in a nutshell. See. I just saved us both a lot of time."

"You make it sound like I was shopping for a pet of some sort."

"I have no idea what you are looking for, Mr. Lawson. But I can tell you, I'm not it." That was pretty much as clear as one could get. Any other man would've walked away long ago, but he didn't budge, didn't even flinch at her words. Was he that thickheaded or just stubborn? Maybe it was because he wasn't getting his way and couldn't stand it. He did seem the type, like most men who stayed here, who believed their money gave them the right to whatever they wanted. She might have been brought up with a silver spoon in her mouth, but those weren't the values her parents instilled in her.

"Maybe if you had dinner with me, you'd find I'm not such a bad guy after all. Well, I do have my moments, but overall, I can be charming. And Mr. Lawson is my father, I like to go by Gareth."

"Fine, Gareth it is. But like I said, you very well might be a nice man, but—"

"You don't like guys with dark hair. Or maybe it's my brown eyes. Or my sense of humor. Too tall maybe? Or was it that I wouldn't go singing? Because that is the one thing I *can* change. What would you like to hear?"

Brooke didn't want to laugh or smile, but she couldn't help it. Once he started singing some country song, belting it out like they were alone on the beach, it was all over.

"You win. You win," she exclaimed.

"So you'll have dinner with me?" he asked, looking hopeful.

"Only if you promise *never* to do that again," she teased.

He grinned. "I told you singing wasn't my thing. Now you know I don't lie. So what time works for you?"

"How about now? I haven't eaten yet."

"It's a bit early for dinner, don't you think?" Gareth asked.

Brooke snorted. "Trying to wiggle out of it again so soon?"

He raised his hands. "Nope. Now is perfect."

"What do you want to eat? I can grab it from the kitchen." It was going to make her feel uncomfortable having any of her coworkers wait on her.

"You can't be serious," Gareth said. "I asked you to eat with me, not serve me."

Before she could reply, Dena, one of the women who worked the front desk, approached. Brooke prepared to be told her mini break had just been cut short. If that was the case, it was okay . . . disappointing, but still okay. She hadn't expected time off in the first place.

"Hi Dena, is Janet looking for me?" she asked.

"No. Actually I'm here for Mr. Lawson. Mr. Henderson said he is ready to meet with you now and then dinner afterward."

Gareth replied, "Can you please let him know I'll reach out when I'm free?"

Brooke stood up. "You can't blow him off. What if he won't meet with you later?" He'd mentioned he was in the steel business. And she understood, work came before pleasure. *Or lunch.*

Dena stood there not sure what to do. Gareth said, "Trust me, he'll see me later. It's either that or you join us for dinner."

Brooke choked. "I think the sun has gotten to you."

"Brooke, I was with Alex last night. That's why I had to cancel our date. I'm not doing that again today. He can wait."

*Date?* Brooke didn't miss the look Dena shot her, but thankfully she didn't verbalize it. *Oh, this is going to bite me in the ass.* "I can't . . ."

Gareth turned toward Dena. "Please tell him I'll call him later this evening."

"Yes sir," Dena replied and scurried away.

"Gareth, this is your business. What if he was ready to give you a huge contract and you just blew it?"

He looked down at her and said, "Then it was his loss. Now, what do you want to eat? I'm thinking mango chicken over wild rice."

Brooke shook her head. "You are so hard to figure out."

Gareth laughed. "If you do, you'll be the first. My brothers have been trying for years."

*I'll be shocked if I even learn your favorite color.* Her expectations were set very low. Not because she didn't think they weren't attracted to each other, but he was here on vacation or business, and she was here to work. It wasn't like they met on some singles cruise or dating site. That didn't mean she wasn't going to enjoy their afternoon together.


Gareth never thought he'd find her lounging on the beach. His intention was to get a feel for the right location for their dinner date. He'd still like to know why she appeared to know nothing about his note. The woman had said she'd get it delivered right away. Had she tossed it instead? Anything was possible. It didn't please him, but since it all seemed to have worked out, he'd let it slip. Besides, that wasn't what he wanted to talk to Alex about tonight. They had much more important things to discuss.

Right now there was something else he wanted to focus on, and that was the beauty sitting beside him. Although the sandy beach wasn't the ideal place to sit and eat, it was at least . . . private. The only intrusion was when the waiter brought their food. Brooke couldn't even look at the man as he laid everything out. He got it, she felt guilty, although she shouldn't. From what he gathered, she'd been working a lot. One afternoon off with a bit of pampering, wasn't much to ask for. So why did she look so . . . uncomfortable sitting there?

"You don't seem to be enjoying yourself," he said.

"I am. It's just weird."

"Being here with me?"

Brooke shrugged. "I guess that too. But mostly breaking the rules and knowing that everyone knows about it."

"Do you really care what anyone thinks?"

Brooke nodded. "I want to leave here with a spotless employment record."

He laughed. "Do you think one lunch with me will do harm? Because I can talk to Alex and let him know this was all my idea. That I gave you no choice and you were forced to spend the afternoon with me."

Her eyes widened. "Don't you dare!"

"Afraid he'll be angry with me?"

Brooke shook her head. "I don't want him to think I'm that weak. If I didn't want to be here, I wouldn't be."

*Good to know.* He didn't try to hide his grin. "So, you do enjoy my company. I knew it."

She wrinkled her nose and curled her lips. "Don't get an inflated ego. It's better than the book I was reading."

That was funny, because he knew exactly who the author was. He wasn't sure if Brooke knew that was Alex's pen name. "Not a fan?"

"No. If I keep reading it, I might not be able to sleep for a month. He is very . . . descriptive."

"I thought that was a good thing in a book."

"Maybe a romance, but not a book like this." He saw her shiver before she continued. "It's so real that when I closed my eyes it felt like I was there. That scared the crap out of me."

"It's only a story," he clarified.

"A very scary one. But you're right, it's ridiculous."

"No. Actually it's a compliment to the author. I'm sure he'd love to hear your feedback." He didn't expect her to follow through with that suggestion, but it hopefully provided her with a different way of looking at the book.

"I never thought of it like that. I'll have to make sure I leave him a good review." She smiled up at him. "Who would've thought you were so thoughtful?"

"Maybe I should help you write the review if that's your way of paying a compliment," he teased.

Brooke laughed. "You're right. I have no idea what it is about you that makes me keep putting my foot in my mouth. My mother would freak out if she heard me."

"Please don't tell me I make you nervous," he begged.

She shook her head. "I'm not afraid of you. Not in the way you might think."

"Do tell. This conversation has piqued my curiosity."

Brooke huffed. "Why do I get the feeling I walked right into that one?" He grinned, playing innocent. "Okay, I'll play. You make me feel . . . uneasy when you look at me." Gareth cocked a brow and looked deep into her beautiful brown eyes. "See. Like that. It's like you're looking into my soul. It . . . it—"

"Scares you?" he asked, not looking away.

"No. Makes me feel . . . vulnerable. I don't normally feel that way."

It wasn't the warm fuzzy feeling he was hoping she'd have, but it meant he stirred something in her that other men hadn't. She was doing the same to him. It'd been a long time since he'd met someone he couldn't stop thinking about. There were a few problems with that. One, he wasn't looking for anything serious. Two, the timing sucked. All she could do right now was fuck with his head so he'd slip up and blow it with Alex.

*Like not meeting with Alex when he just asked me.*

Hopefully he'd iron that out with Alex later. There was no doubt in his mind that Dena would've reported the reason behind Gareth's delay. Was Alex going to be understanding or an ass? Gareth had no idea. A part of him didn't give a shit. But Alex seemed to be willing to talk, and that was something Brice hadn't been willing to do. Gareth needed to move while the opportunity was still there.

Gareth couldn't end his lunch with Brooke on that note. He wanted her to know she wasn't the only one feeling that way. Yet he couldn't make any promises. Not even that he'd have time to see her tomorrow.

"I find myself wanting to spend more time with you. Maybe more time than I have. I wish things were different, but that's the facts. I'm here on business and . . . I find myself not wanting to leave for my meeting."

That said more than he wanted, but her eyes softened when he said it, so she got his point.

"Well, Mr. Henderson wouldn't be too happy with me either if you decide to cancel all together. Although I have a strange feeling we're going to be seeing each other again very soon."

"Do you know something I don't?" he asked.

Those beautiful lips of hers curled as she said, "Yes. I'm on the schedule tomorrow for room service, and if I'm right, you'll be ordering your usual. Two eggs, two bacon strips, two sausage links, and extra coffee."

He laughed. "That's not fair."

"What isn't?"

"You know more about me than I do about you. I guess

we're going to have to do dinner tomorrow night to rectify that."

Brooke rolled her eyes. "Please no more dinner invites. They don't seem to work for us."

He leaned over and said softly, "Trust me, Brooke. I won't ever stand you up again. And if something delays me, I'll let you know personally."

She swallowed hard and replied, "Don't make promises, Gareth. Neither of us is in the position to keep them."

"Sweet Brooke, there are many things I can control, and where I am and who I spend time with is one of them. I promise, I'll be in the lobby tomorrow at six waiting for you." He kissed her lightly before she could argue. "But right now, I'm going to heed your advice and go meet with Alex."

He could tell she was flustered by his brief kiss, but she didn't say a word about it. "Good luck," she said as he stood up.

"Are you staying here on the beach?" he asked.

Brooke nodded. "Actually I'm going to give this book another try. Who knows, maybe it'll grow on me."

*Like you have grown on me.*

"If you can't sleep, you know what room I'm in." He gave her playful wink before turning to head back to the hotel. He knew damn well she wouldn't show up, but he wouldn't turn her away if she did. Distraction or not, he wanted her.

*This trip is full of surprises. Wish they were all as sweet as Brooke.*

His next stop was Alex's office. It wasn't as informal as dinner had been last night, but they had more privacy, which seemed more important at the moment.

"Before we begin, how is it you knew who I am and why I'm here?" Gareth asked.

Alex said, "I didn't. But Bennett Stone, my brother-in-law, keeps a close eye on who travels to Tabiq. When your name crossed the roster, he suggested I return to Tabiq immediately."

"He believes I'm a threat?"

Alex shook his head. "If that was the case, he'd be here as well as his team. But he makes a point of knowing more about our family than we'd like him to."

"Meaning the reason I'm here," Gareth said flatly.

"Exactly. I will have to admit, this has come as a shock to me as well. I've been one of the family members who *didn't* want to learn anything more about our father or his parents. But that has changed."

"Because of Audrey?"

"She has always been a concern, but now more than ever. Unfortunately both our families are part of a club we wish we weren't in."

He wasn't sure what club that was. "What the hell does that mean?" Alex leaned back in his leather chair and stared at Gareth for what seemed like an eternity. He knew Alex wanted to tell him, but was holding back. So he pushed. "I could be out enjoying my day with—"

"Yes. One of my employees. So I've heard. We'll talk about that later. Right now, I'm trying to figure out where to start or more importantly where to end."

"Maybe it'd help if I told you what I know so far." Alex agreed and Gareth spent the next hour sharing everything Brice had told them and then added more of what his family life had been. Alex didn't seem shocked at all as Gareth talked about their great-granddad and what he did to Aunt Audrey. "What has me puzzled is what Tabiq has to do with it all. I know your father came here and participated in some very . . . disgusting things. But why are you all here? I would think the last thing you'd want would be to step foot on this soil. Hell, I wouldn't think they'd want you here either."

Alex said, "You know more than I expected. And actually, you've enlightened me to things I wasn't aware of. Seems my brother Brice still tries to control shit."

"He said it is to protect the family," Gareth corrected. *I know what he means. I'm doing the same thing.*

"Who is he to determine what any of us have the right to know? I knew my grandmother was fucked up. Hell, it explains a lot about my father too. But no one informed me they believed she killed her husband's first wife. Not that this should surprise me. From what I already knew about her, pure evil ran through her veins, not blood."

"I'm sure what Great-granddad did to her didn't help any. If anything, it probably magnified the problem. Hate and resentment are powerful tools and can be very destructive in the hands of someone . . . unstable."

"And now we're left with the cleanup," Alex said with a heavy look on his face.

"What does New Hope have to do with what your father did?"

"Seems Brice left out a large piece. I get it. It's personal and fucking ugly as hell. No one would want such things about their family exposed. But you're family. And unfortunately, your family is involved. I hope you don't have any plans for tonight, because it's going to be a long evening. I let Ziva know I won't be home till very late."

Since it wasn't even dinner time, what Alex was about to say might be more than Gareth was ready to hear. But would he ever be ready? He'd come this far for this information. Just because it wasn't something pleasant, didn't mean he should walk away. In his gut, he'd always known it wasn't good. *Nothing about Aunt Audrey has been.*

"I want to know it all. If takes all week, I don't care."

"Before we start, I want to remind you, this information could destroy my family. I'm trusting you with it because how closely linked you are to it as well."

"I'm here because I believe we can't protect our families by turning a blind eye to the past. That is what got us all in this problem in the first place." If Great-granddad hadn't ignored what was going on with Aunt Audrey, their lives would all be different. *Hell, we might not even exist.*

"Okay. So let's start with exactly what went on here in Tabiq. My father was a very sick and cruel man, but he wasn't the only one. There were men willing to back him financially, so they could all achieve greater wealth. That includes a Lawson as well."

"Brice had mentioned something about that. He didn't go into any details. Probably because he didn't want us to know what happened here."

"My brother and I handle things differently. He holds it all in and tries to control it that way. I, on the other hand, think of my family history when I'm at my laptop writing a horrific scene. No matter how gruesome I make it, I know my father and grandmother did worse."

Gareth nodded. "Unfortunately I understand that all too well. So tell me everything, and then maybe I'll understand what I, I mean we Lawsons, need to do in order to fix it."

"Fix it? That won't happen. All we can do is try to build Tabiq back up to a place where it will be strong enough not to fall prey to assholes like—"

"Us. Damn it, Alex. That is the underlying fear, isn't it? That one day we learn we're just as fucked up as they were." It was something he'd seen in Dylan's eyes when he learned he was about to become a father. No one wanted to pass this legacy on to their children. Gareth wasn't one who had to worry about that, but he hated knowing it weighed on his brothers' minds.

"I think we all go through that, but as time goes by, we all have come to the understanding that we make our own paths. We're not saying we can ever forget, but we refuse to let their actions define us as individuals. Since this is all fresh to you guys, you'll need to go through that process just like we did."

"You mean the one where you wish you were born into a different family? Because that's how it's starting to feel." The Lawson name, one he'd been so proud of, now felt like a noose tightening around his neck. *And Charles worried that Dylan and I would be the ones who'd tarnish the family name. Ha. No scandal I've been in could touch this shit.*

"That is why New Hope means so much to us. And it's not just the resort. There are schools, hospitals, and a police force that doesn't report to the highest bidder. All this is what has made it possible for us to move forward with our lives. Happy ones by the way. And I believe the Lawsons will too. If you choose to, that is."

From what he saw the night before, Alex and Ziva were definitely happy. He could see his family starting to be the same. But they weren't over the hurdles yet. "It's my hope we do too. So, why don't you start by telling me what our families really did to this country."

The next several hours were spent learning what the ugly side of wealth could do. That night he wouldn't be able to close his eyes without seeing the faces of the Tabiqian people who worked there. He'd thought James Henderson had been the only one involved in the human trafficking. Never had he imagined James and his great-granddad had actually started it in Tabiq. *Two brilliant businessmen who had everything but a heart and soul.*

He knew he needed to check in with Dylan, but he didn't

want to chat that night. Instead he sent him a quick text so he wouldn't be concerned.

ALL IS FINE. MET WITH ALEX. NICE GUY. WILL TELL YOU ABOUT IT WHEN I RETURN TO THE STATES.

Dylan replied: IS THIS A GOOD THING?

*It can be.* Meeting with Alex had provided one thing. Hope. Even though the Hendersons couldn't change the past, they also didn't run from it. Alex promised to take him around and give him a private tour of the inner workings of Tabiq within the next few days. That was the information he wanted to take back to his family. How this generation could make a difference as well. *A positive one.*

IT'S A VERY GOOD THING. I'LL BE BACK NEXT WEEK.

Dylan asked: WHY SO LONG?

NOW I'M TAKING A VACATION.

He'd promised Brooke he wouldn't stand her up, and he meant it. Besides, he wanted to get to know her better. *And taste those sweet lips of hers again.*

What was it about Tabiq? Was everything an extreme? Even his desire to be near her, never mind with her, was more than he'd felt with any other woman. Gareth was going to need to tread carefully with this one. All the stress and tension in Tabiq had to be clouding his judgment. What he felt for her was nothing more than a strong sexual attraction. Lust didn't rule him. And he wasn't about to give in to it.

*The last thing I want to do is fuck with anyone here in Tabiq. As if we outsiders haven't done enough already.*

It was funny, she looked like she was born there, dark hair, dark eyes, beautiful olive skin, but her accent wasn't right. He needed to ask her where she was from. Then again, did he really want to get to know her more personally than he already did?

*Personally? Yes. Intimately? Fuck yeah!* Neither was going to happen. So why the hell was he chasing her if he had no intention of following through? *Cause she's irresistible.* It was a good thing he wasn't going to be in Tabiq much longer. Being around her could become a habit. One he didn't want. One that was going to be hard to break.

## 5

She didn't need to tell Janet that Gareth kissed her. It wasn't like a real kiss. Well it was a real kiss but not one that . . . *Hell, it was so a real kiss.* It might have been brief, but her entire body ached for more. She didn't understand why he'd kissed her.

It was stupid to overthink it, but that seemed to be what women did best. Women thought too much and men thought too little. Gareth probably hadn't given it a second thought after he left her yesterday. Of course he was off meeting with the big boss. She really hoped it went well for him. Gareth seemed like an okay guy, minus the fact that he wasn't exactly reliable. *Maybe just on dates but with business he's spot on.*

She laughed to herself. When she thought about him, the only steel she was thinking about were his abs. *And biceps. And pecs. Damn he's solid.* Through that T-shirt he'd worn, she could see every muscle flex. It was hot in the sun, and she almost suggested he take it off, but that would only make it hotter for her.

Had it been that long? Was that why every time she

bumped into Gareth, she found herself horny? That wasn't like her at all. She did enjoy sex, very much, but she wasn't one whose blood pumped with something as simple as a peck on the lips. Yet Gareth had accomplished that. Maybe that was why she opted to dress a bit differently this time.

Taking one last look in the mirror, she knew he wasn't going to be prepared for her. She'd taken the time to straighten her long dark hair so it shined like silk. He'd never seen her with makeup either. Not that she wore much, but enough mascara to make her eyes pop and a hint of lipstick to entice. She only had one dress, a form-fitting black one that fell off her shoulders. With matching stilettos she felt pretty, but with the black strapless bra and thong she felt sexy as sin.

Gareth called and said they were going to dinner off the resort. Since she'd never been anywhere but New Hope, she had no idea what to expect. So she dressed up instead of dressing down. Hopefully she nailed it. She'd know soon as she headed to meet him in the lobby.

She took the elevator, and when the door opened another employee got inside too. He looked at her and asked, "Brooke?"

"Yes. It's me," she replied. By the look on his face, the change was significant. This was the way she dressed back home. There was always some event or occasion that required dressing up. But it was expected at home. Here all she needed was her waitress uniform and shorts for when she was off the clock.

"You look . . . different," he stammered.

"Thank you." Brooke hoped he'd meant it as a compliment.

When the doors opened and she stepped out, she strutted out with confidence. There was only one head she wanted to turn, but really, what woman complained about turning more than one?

She held her breath as she turned the corner where Gareth should be waiting for her. Would he find her attractive too? She hoped so. This was all for him. When she arrived in the lobby, his back was to her, and she could tell he was on the phone. *So much for a grand entrance.* She could step back around the corner and try again, but why bother? She didn't believe in forcing things. If he was meant to see her and be blown away, he'd have been looking in her direction.

Brooke made her way to him and tapped him on the shoulder. Gareth, with the phone to his ear, turned. His eyes roamed over her, head to toe, nice and slow.

"Dylan, I've got to go. Something's come up." Gareth didn't seem to wait for a response as he slipped his phone into his pocket. "I'm sorry miss, but I'm waiting for someone. Don't know if you've seen her. She's a waitress here by the name of Brooke."

Since he was wearing a suit jacket, she had chosen well. Brooke smiled and stepped closer. "Would you rather I go and change?"

He shook his head. "I thought you were beautiful the first time I saw you, but this dress . . . well it makes me want to skip dinner and . . ."

"Oh no you don't. You promised me you wouldn't cancel again," Brook warned.

"I'm sorry. I guess the blood flow to my brain was temporarily interrupted." He gave her a playful wink then added, "Dinner it is. Maybe I should've been clear as to where we're going."

"Anywhere is fine with me. I'm looking forward to leaving the resort for a while." *And being with you.*

"Then you'll enjoy where we are going."

"Good. I love surprises," she said.

"Really? I hate them," Gareth said then added, "because they never are as good as you look."

She blushed slightly, which was funny. Brooke wasn't one who blushed easily. Was it the way he looked at her? Or maybe what he said? More likely it was her own thoughts, as she was tempted to tell him they could skip dinner because dessert was so much sweeter. They hadn't known each other long enough to even think about . . . sex. Yet, it was as though he was eating her up with his eyes, and her body betrayed her, wanting more.

The night was young and she wasn't about to waste the opportunity to see someplace besides New Hope. And although her body might disagree, she wasn't ready to take the next step with Gareth. She was still trying to figure him out. Realistically, he'd probably be gone before she did.

She wasn't going to think about him leaving, not when they had a lovely night ahead of them. Brooke could live in the moment, and this was one she didn't want to miss. *Hopefully he has a romantic dinner for two planned. Someplace private, with a view.*

"Gareth, I hope standing in the lobby wasn't the plan," she teased.

He laughed. "No. But once again, I'm blaming you. You really took my breath away when I turned around."

*Nailed it.* "Thank you," she smiled sweetly. "It feels nice to have a reason to dress up." She tapped her foot lightly and added, "Which, by the way, is the hint for us to go, because I'm famished."

He laughed. "Oh, don't worry, I picked up on it." With a wicked grin he added, "And before you ask, it wasn't the sound of your growling stomach that gave it away."

"That's horrible, my stomach wasn't—"

"I know. It's mine. I'm starving too." He reached for her hand, and she slipped hers in his. "And at this point, I think we're going to be late."

As they made their way out of the door, she asked, "What time is our reservation?"

"I thought you liked surprises," Gareth said, opening the back door of the waiting black SUV.

"I didn't think knowing a time was going to ruin it," she chuckled.

Inside he tapped the driver that they were ready. When they pulled away from New Hope, Gareth turned and said, "It's kind of complicated."

"Dinner or the time?"

"I love how quick-witted you are. I hope your sense of humor continues when I tell you where we are going."

"Let me guess, you've charted a plane and are stealing me off to some deserted island." Of course Tabiq was quite beautiful, just . . . poor.

"Nothing quite that elaborate. We're having dinner with . . . friends."

Brooke turned to him. "I hate to break it to you, but I don't have any friends here. Not that I'm unfriendly, but the people of Tabiq like to keep to themselves."

"Not all of them," Gareth stated.

*Great. I'm here ten months and nothing. He's here a week and has already been invited out.* "So we are going to meet *your* friends at a restaurant?"

"No. We're going to their home."

Brooke started to panic. This was a bad idea. She hadn't told anyone she was leaving with Gareth, and he was taking her to God-knows-where. She could only imagine the riot act she was going to receive from Janet when she fessed up. Was it too late to change her mind? Gareth surely wouldn't force her to go with him if she asked to return to New Hope.

That was the issue. She had no idea what he was capable of. So far she was letting her libido drive her actions. Stupid. Very stupid. Someone as world traveled as she was, knew better. Her heart raced and she tensed. Gareth must have noticed because he asked, "Are you okay?"

This was her chance. She could tell him she had a headache, or felt queasy, or . . . or . . . *just tell him the truth.* "Gareth, I'm not comfortable with this."

"With what? Us having dinner together?"

She shook her head. "There are reasons we're told not to leave the resort. I'm sure your friends are very nice, but this is still . . . unwise."

"I'll have the driver turn around if that is what you want. But do you really believe I'd take you someplace you might not be completely safe?" He waited until she shook her head before he continued. "I'm glad. Because you have my word, Brooke, I'd never let anything happen to you."

"Okay," she said meekly. She wanted to believe that, but not knowing was unnerving.

"Would you feel better if I told you where we are headed?"

Brooke had told him she enjoyed surprises. Then she freaked out because he was doing just that. Should she go for three and change her mind once again? If she followed her head, she'd still have him take her back to New Hope no matter where they were headed. But her heart said she could trust him. *Following one's heart usually leads to one thing. Heartbreak. God, I hope I don't regret this.*

"No. But I'm telling you, if something happens to me, you'll have to answer to Janet."

"Who is Janet?" Gareth asked.

"My boss. She lives here on the island with her husband, Vinny. They are both from the States, but fell in love with Tabiq. Go figure. I'm not allowed off the resort, and she lives here." She gave a nervous laugh.

"Why is that funny?"

"First of all, I look like I could be a native here, which I'm not. But she has a mass of blonde curls. Definitely not Tabiqian."

"So where are you from?" Gareth asked.

"Originally or now?"

"How about both?"

"I was born in Panama. When I was eight, my parents moved to Canada. When I was twelve, we moved to the States. That's why I love moving around so much now. How about you?"

"Born and raised in New York. Although I love to travel, I'm a city boy."

"Really? I pictured you more of the ranch-hand type," she teased.

"You couldn't pay me to muck a stall."

"I actually did that one year."

"And you liked it?" Gareth asked.

Brooke wrinkled her nose. "I loved the horses; does that count?"

"Were you on community service or something?" Gareth joked.

"No. Actually I try something new and different every year. This year I'm waitressing at a resort. I've waitressed a few places, but the locations have all been different."

"You mean you can't commit to anything longer than twelve months?" He arched a brow.

That sounded too much like what her friends had asked

her. "I can, but why? Think about the endless possibilities. The world is a big place and I want to see it."

"I'm glad you found a way to see it. But isn't that . . . dangerous? I mean you going off to all these strange places alone?"

Brooke knew it sounded odd. And if Gareth knew her family, it would sound more ridiculous. But she rarely let anyone know who she was. Otherwise they might not hire her. At least not in the jobs she'd applied for. All she needed was room and board and enough of a wage to keep her stable for the year. Someone like Gareth definitely wouldn't understand.

"Trust me. I do plenty of research. Going out with you is probably the riskiest thing I've done in a long time." She thought about how that sounded. His expression didn't show that it bothered him at all.

"I'm glad to hear it. And you're right. Knowing what you can and shouldn't do in a strange country is what will keep you safe. If you weren't out with me right now, I wouldn't advise leaving the resort either."

"So everyone says, but no one actually says anything more than that. I'm a rule follower. Well, for the most part I am. You seem to bring out the—"

"Naughty side?" He winked.

"I wouldn't go that far. And for the record, I let my boss know we were having dinner. There may have been a few details left out, but she knows."

"Good, because I don't kiss and tell either."

*Kiss. Yeah. Never mentioned that.* Brooke smiled. If she was lucky, there would be more of that later. *They are so worth breaking the rules for.*

She hadn't been paying attention to where they were

67

going, but when they turned up a long driveway, she had to ask. "Your friend's house?"

"Yes."

"Who exactly are they?"

"Alex and Ziva Henderson."

Brooke sucked in a deep breath. "I can't be here. We're not supposed to be dating. And I never told anyone I was leaving. Oh shit. I'm going to get fired. I need you to take me back right now, please."

Gareth chuckled and took her hand in his. "One, you're not getting fired. Two, they are expecting *us*. And I think you're allowed to leave New Hope when the owner invites you to dinner, don't you think?"

*I wouldn't have dressed sexy if I'd have known.* "I'd like to change my answer."

"To what question?" Gareth asked.

"Whether or not I like surprises."

He brought her hand to his lips and placed a gentle kiss on her fingers. "Okay. I'll remember that next time. Now let's go before the children drive them crazy and they eat without us."

*Kids?* She knew she was definitely overdressed now. *And that's what I get for not doing my research like I normally do.*

Gareth didn't even need to knock on the door. Charisa was already pulling it open. "I've been waiting for you all day."

He laughed. "I thought you had school."

Charisa giggled. "Yes, but I have been waiting for at least five minutes." Then she peered around him and saw Brooke. "You're not a little girl."

Gareth said, "I said I was bringing a friend. This is Brooke. Brooke this is Charisa."

Charisa pouted. "I thought she was going to want to play with me. I have a new dolly and no one to play with."

Brooke bent over and said, "What is your dolly's name?"

Charisa smiled. "Dolly. Want to see her?" She reached out for Brooke's hand and led her inside.

Alex and Ziva were standing behind Charisa for the entire exchange. Ziva said, "Charisa, you know you can't play with your doll until after dinner. Besides, I'm sure Gareth and Brooke are hungry."

"Oh Mommy. I'm not hungry, and I don't think Rookie is either."

Alex said, "Her name is Brooke, not Rookie, and you heard your mother. Dolls after dinner."

Charisa didn't let Brooke's hand go and said, "Then follow me and eat fast. Even your veggies." She half dragged Brooke across the hall.

Brooke turned, wide-eyed, and said, "Good thing I'm hungry."

They all followed behind. Charisa held out Brooke's chair for her and waited until she sat down. Then she turned to Gareth and said, "You can sit over there in my seat. I want to sit next to Rookie. She's my friend now. You can have Mommy and Daddy."

They all burst out laughing. Gareth winked at Brooke and said, "You can have Rookie now, but she is coming home with me."

Charisa pouted again. "Then no dessert or we won't have any time to play." She turned to Brooke and asked, "Do you like broccoli?"

"I do," she replied.

"Can you eat mine and I'll eat your potatoes?" In a low voice she added, "But don't let Mommy see you or she'll give us more."

Ziva rolled her eyes. "Is this what I'm in for when Nikko gets older?"

Gareth and Alex shook their heads and Alex said, "No. It's worst with boys."

"How can that be?"

Gareth added, "Girls talk a lot and boys break everything. Somehow we look at it and it falls apart."

Charisa said, "Oh no. Nikko isn't touching my dollies." Then she turned to her mother and asked, "Can we trade him for a sister?"

Ziva shook her head. Brooke leaned over and whispered something in Charisa's ear. Charisa giggled again and said. "Okay, we can keep him."

They all looked at Brooke, wishing they knew what she'd just said, but Gareth was glad she was able to make things all better. At least for the time being.

The rest of the meal was more talk about Tabiq than anything else. Gareth watched Brooke, who seemed to be soaking up every word. It was as though she wanted to know as much about the culture as possible. He understood why they normally didn't speak of it, but he was surprised they spoke in front of Charisa.

There were a lot of details left out, mostly around the abuse, but a lot was discussed. When Charisa ran off to play, totally forgetting about Brooke, Gareth had to ask. "You aren't worried that Charisa will be afraid to live here?"

Ziva shook her head. "I have lived here all my life. As a child we were told of the risk of growing up as a girl in this country. The only way to ensure we do not revert back to those days is to raise our children with the truth. Knowledge gives us power. And Charisa and the others are the future. They need to understand the past so they don't repeat the mistakes."

Gareth could tell Ziva knew exactly what those mistakes were. Both from their visits and from what Alex had shared with him. It blew his mind that Ziva could actually marry into the family that had practically sold her country into slavery. Yet even as they sat together, he felt no resentment from her toward Alex. Her acceptance of him was shocking.

*If the Tabiqian people can forgive the Henderson and Lawson families, why can't we forgive each other?* It wasn't what had happened that stood in the way, it was that his family still didn't know what really had transpired. Ziva was correct. There was power in knowledge and right now, the Lawson family felt powerless. As soon as he returned to the States, that needed to be rectified. Of course lying to most of the family and coming here by himself wasn't going to make him popular with them for a while. But Gareth knew he'd do something else soon enough to piss them off. He always did.

He turned his attention back to Ziva and said, "I wish my granddad had made that decision. It might have stopped all this sooner."

"Gareth, we have no idea what would've happened. My brothers and I have questioned things ourselves. What if we had rebelled against the big bad James Henderson when we were young? Or what if my grandmother wasn't such a cruel evil woman? There are so many what-ifs, but none of them change what was."

Ziva nodded and reached over to cover Alex's hand with hers. "Or more importantly, what is now. Because that's all we have. This moment and hope for the next. One thing about growing up in Tabiq, it made you appreciate what you have, because focusing on what you didn't was pointless."

"Seems like Tabiq is a lot stronger than most people give it credit for," Gareth said.

"Yes it is. But I'm sure you didn't bring your date here to

71

talk about my country all night. I'd much rather hear about her," Ziva said. "I heard enough about Gareth the last time he was here. So tell me, how do you like working at New Hope?"

Brooke smiled. "I'm loving it. You have a top notch resort. I'm going to miss it when I'm gone."

"Janet told me you didn't want to sign on for another year. Is there a reason why?" Alex asked.

"No. It's just I . . . well I . . ."

"She likes to travel. What better way to see the world," Gareth answered for her. She had no problem explaining it to him, but found it odd that she didn't feel comfortable doing the same with them.

"One adventure after another sounds like a lot of fun. I did that for a long time. If you read my books, you'll see that is how I decided on the settings for each story," Alex said.

"You definitely know how to make someone feel like they are living in the story. You're an amazing author," Brooke said.

Gareth didn't realize she knew who was behind that pen name. But Brooke still didn't know Gareth and Alex were related. So far they'd only introduced each other as friends. Neither were ready to admit to anything more. If so, it would open them up to questions no one wanted. It wasn't like time was going to change that. The less people that knew the better. Yet there he was with Brooke. What the hell made him think bringing her with him was a good idea? Of course she seemed to be enjoying herself. And Ziva seemed to love having female company as well. Although the one thing they hadn't talked about tonight was business. Supposedly that's why he'd been at New Hope. Brooke wasn't one who missed much. She had to have noticed there was more going on than he and Alex let on.

*And then I'll have to start lying. That sucks.*

"Alex, why don't we let these two head out early? I mean, I'm sure they have something better to do than sit here with us all night. And besides, you promised Charisa you'd read her a story before bed."

Gareth had to admit, he was glad Ziva suggested they leave. It saved him from coming up with an excuse to go.

"Thank you again for having us over for dinner," Gareth said.

Brooke added, "I never imagined this was where Gareth was taking me tonight. But it was a very pleasant surprise. You have a lovely daughter. Please let her know, next time, I'll bring my dolly with me."

Ziva chuckled. "She has more energy than all four of us put together. If you show up with a doll, I think you'll be held prisoner for hours upstairs."

"Growing up as an only child, I remember how much I wanted someone to play with. So if you don't mind, I'd really enjoy returning sometime. Maybe not for hours, but just to keep my promise to her," Brooke said.

Alex replied, "You both are welcome any time."

Somehow knowing that Brooke was welcome anytime at the Henderson home eased his mind a bit about leaving her behind in Tabiq. It wasn't as though anything was going to happen to her, but he was glad Alex and Ziva would be there to keep an eye on her for him.

On the way back to the resort, Brooke seemed much more relaxed than earlier. She sat closer than before. Not as close as he'd like, but that might be for the best. It wasn't like they could do anything on the bumpy road back.

"Did you enjoy yourself?" he asked.

She turned to him and said, "It was really nice. But then again, I seem to enjoy myself anytime I'm with you."

"Does that mean I can talk you into having a nightcap with me when we get back?" Gareth needed to make sure she understood what he was offering. "I know those shoes aren't great on the beach, but there is a comfortable lounge that serves some awesome tropical drinks."

He was more of a bourbon guy, but if it meant this night not ending, he'd have one of those fancy fruity umbrella drinks.

"I'd really like that, but you do know I have to work in the morning."

Gareth was trying to forget that. "So you're saying only one drink?"

She laughed and slid a bit closer to him. "I'm saying only two."

Even though this night wasn't going to end in his bed, he was glad it wasn't ending soon.

## 6

Last night had been amazing. Although she learned more about Tabiq in a few hours than she had in the past ten months, the best part was her time alone with Gareth afterward. It wasn't like they did a lot of talking; they just sat in the lounge and listened to music. She enjoyed his company most of all.

How could sitting and not speaking be so nice? What wasn't pleasant was the headache she was fighting this morning. The staff knew she didn't drink alcohol, so they'd brought her virgin frozen Hopeless In Love drinks both times. Absolutely delicious, they were a mix of coconut and pineapple. Unless someone knew what extra cherries around the fancy umbrella meant, they'd never know the difference.

Yet the pounding in her temple wasn't going away. She knew it was from lack of sleep. Brooke had intended to only spend an hour with him listening to music. Somehow the time slipped away, and before she knew it the clock showed two in the morning. For someone who had to get up at five, that really sucked. But here she was, dressed and at least looking ready to wait on whoever was hungry while all she wanted to do was crawl back under the covers and sleep all day.

If her morning wasn't starting rough already, Janet was there and not looking too pleased either. She didn't normally arrive until seven at the earliest, so this had to be bad. The fact she was headed in Brooke's direction was a good indication it had to do with her.

*I knew there was going to be a price to pay for last night.*

"Good morning, Brooke. Could you please come with me to my office?"

Brooke nodded and followed her out of the dining area and down the hall. She sensed all the staff staring. She knew she would be the topic of gossip today. Not that any was ever shared with her, but she knew it would be about her. And well deserved too.

Once inside, Janet closed the door and said, "Have a seat." Brooke did as she instructed and waited. Once Janet sat down at her desk, she said, "You put me in a very difficult situation. I have no choice but to bring you into my office."

"I understand. The policy is in place for a reason." Brooke felt horrible. In all her life, she'd never had the smallest blemish on her record. This wasn't an accident. She had full control over what she did and didn't do with Gareth. She fully knew and understood what could happen by ignoring the rules.

Janet leaned over and peered at Brooke. She waited to hear she was suspended or fired or had to sign a written warning. But Janet just kept looking at her instead.

"I wish I could say more. I'm guilty," Brooke confessed.

"You better believe you are. And do you know what gets me the most?" Brooke shook her head. "I had to overhear the staff talking about it. I would've thought you'd have mentioned something about it to me."

Brooke blinked. Janet's expression wasn't angry. So what was it? "I guess I wasn't thinking about that at the time."

"No. And now I'm forced to drag you into my office and keep you here for a bit so everyone thinks you're being reprimanded."

"I'm not?" Brooke asked, fully confused.

"You think I'm going to write you a warning for sneaking off New Hope and having dinner with one of the owners and his family? I might as well fire myself." Janet laughed.

"I'm not in here to get . . ."

"You're in here to make it *look* like you're in trouble. And maybe to spill some of the good details I'm dying to hear."

Brooke smirked. "Details? I believe you already know the Hendersons."

Janet rolled her eyes and picked up her pen. "It's not too late, you know," she teased. They both knew it was an empty threat.

"Oh, you mean Mr. Lawson."

"Of course I do. And with the dress you wore, I don't think you call him Mr. Lawson any longer. I heard you turned quite a few heads last night. You'll have to tell me where you got it."

"It's so old, I can't remember. But I brought it along just in case there ever was an occasion I needed to—"

"Sexy it up?" Janet asked. She nodded. "And did Gareth like the dress?"

"Oh yes. And if I had known he was taking me to Alex and Ziva's home, I would've worn something else."

"Are you kidding me? Ziva was the one who texted me last night about the dress. She loved it too. By the way, they really liked you. Ziva's exact words were: You need to find a way to get her to stay in Tabiq."

Brooke laughed. "You better pick up that pen again,

because that's not happening. It's nothing against Tabiq or anyplace. I just enjoy traveling. That's why I wanted only a one-year contract with New Hope."

"I get it. You're single and young, and it's your time to live your life. But don't you ever think about settling down? You know, getting married and having a family?"

"Of course I do. But I work so much and with my life-style, I can't see that happening any time soon." And she wasn't looking for it either. Her parents might be thrilled, but she wasn't so sure about that either.

"You don't plan that. It just happens. I told you the way I met Vinny."

"Yes you did, maybe ten times," Brooke teased. "By the way, it's a very romantic story. I think you should write a book about it someday."

Janet laughed. "I'm no author."

"No, but I bet Vinny would be happy to give you a lot of material for that book." Brooke loved watching Janet blush. It was nice to see happily married couples. Some of her friends had married. Happy was not a word she would use to describe them. Then again, their reason for marriage wasn't the same either. It was all about status and money. Joining forces to create an empire. But where was the love? The passion? Nope. Only dollar signs. Maybe that was what kept Brooke moving around so much. She didn't want to end up like them.

"Just remember, this romantic love story you're talking about wasn't planned. They never are. One minute you're happy in your life and not looking to change a thing, then bam, some sexy man comes along and sweeps you off your feet. You don't even know it's happening until it's too late. You're in love."

Brooke leaned back in her chair. She didn't get enough

sleep for all this . . . joyfulness so early. "Janet, how did we get on this subject?"

"You were telling me about Gareth, and I guess I was—"

"Running off on a tangent and about to plan my wedding. I think I'd rather have the written warning right now." Brooke snickered.

"Don't try to pretend like you're not interested in him. I've seen the way you look at him."

Brooke crossed her arms. "I don't remember ever bumping into you when we were together."

"Exactly. Because when you're with him, the world around you seems to vanish. It was a few days ago, and you were on the beach. I gave you the afternoon off. I worried that you might not be heeding my advice and actually relaxing. I was wrong. You two were all cozy on the blanket."

"We were having lunch."

"I saw that. But trust me, Brooke, I see people all the time. You like him. Why won't you admit it?"

*Because it doesn't matter. He's leaving.* "Janet, I'm not here to meet someone."

"And?"

"And I don't believe he is either." That was the truth. It wasn't as though he asked her to his room last night. She would've said no, but he could've tried. *I want him to want me so I can say no? That's so screwed up.* No, that wasn't it. She was afraid of getting attached. Then when he left, it would hurt like hell. It was better not to know what she would be missing.

"For someone so well-traveled, you are horrible with relationships."

"I've dated."

"But when was the last time you dated someone like Gareth?"

"I don't—"

"Date handsome sexy men? Why?" Janet asked.

"No. I don't date men with money," Brooke blurted.

Janet cocked her head. "I wasn't prepared for that response. You want someone broke?"

"No. It's complicated."

"So it seems. Let me get this straight. You don't want to date him because he's rich?"

"When you say it like that, it sounds stupid," Brooke stated.

"Yes it does. Glad you realize that. So what do you have against people with money?"

"I don't have anything against people with money; I just don't want to date them. Love has nothing to do with material things. Money clutters it up, and when it's gone, sometimes you find there's nothing left."

"I can see your point. So you'd rather have nothing, so you can't lose it?"

"No, but my love is not for sale." She'd received many expensive gifts over the years. They meant nothing to her, because they'd been no effort for the guy to obtain. It would've meant more for someone to put a quarter in a gumball machine and win a cheap plastic ring for her. Same sentiment, but it wasn't about showing off. *I don't need bling. I need heart.*

"I get it now. You are looking for the real thing, just afraid you won't find it. So you shut it down before you can be disappointed."

Brooke sat back and thought about that statement. It wasn't really hard to see how Janet was able to deduce that from this conversation. She had dressed up last night for Gareth, wanting his attention. It wasn't like she'd thrown herself at him, but it was clear she was interested. That didn't fit with what Janet said. Not really. Doing all this for a man she knew was going to be leaving didn't mean anything. It just meant there were no expectations for anything afterward, that's all.

*Damn it. That's exactly why I'm doing this. Because I know it can't go anywhere.* But she did like him more than she wanted to admit. If he didn't leave soon, that feeling might develop into something she didn't want. The last thing she wanted was to find the real thing with someone who didn't feel the same way.

"I guess it's a good thing there's a policy about dating the guests then. I don't have to worry about falling in love." *And getting my heart broken.*

"That's a good defense. Doesn't change anything. You still like him. And this is going to make it harder for you: Alex said he had no issue with you dating him. So there you go. No excuses. What are you going to do now?" Janet asked, looking quite pleased with herself.

Brooke didn't understand why Alex would change the policy based on one guest. She had to be missing something. She thought they had just met and were business associates. Yet last night she picked up on something more. Janet's comment only confirmed it. Was it worth looking into? *Yes, since it seems to now include me.*

She asked, "Janet, you don't find that odd?"

Janet shrugged. "Nothing in Tabiq surprises me anymore."

Brooke wasn't concerned about Tabiq. Gareth had her puzzled. Why exactly was he here? Granted, he was full of mystery, and she was slowly getting to know him. After last night's after-dinner conversation, Brooke understood why the Hendersons were so protective of Tabiq. Was Gareth here to help rebuild the country? God knows the Lawson family has the assets and money to do it. Maybe he wasn't leaving Tabiq for long. That would explain the extended job offer from Ziva too.

She had to agree with Janet. Tabiq was full of surprises. But she had one for all of them. She wasn't extending her contract. She might like it here, but she was leaving in two months, and it was going to be a one-way ticket.

There was a knock on the door and Brooke was thrilled for the interruption. Janet called out for them to enter.

"Excuse me, but there is a problem in the kitchen. One of the pipes has broken and water is spraying everywhere."

"Oh no. Did you shut off the water to the kitchen?"

"We don't know how," the man exclaimed.

Janet got up from behind the desk, and they all dashed to the dining room. Water was shooting out of the sprinkler pipe on the ceiling. She turned to Brooke and asked, "Do you know what to do?"

Brooke knew nothing about construction. So she pulled out her cell and rang Gareth's number. She blurted out what was happening and he said he'd be right there.

"Who did you call?" Janet asked as she watched the water.

"Gareth."

Janet turned to her and said, "A guest?"

When she had dialed the number Brooke wasn't thinking of him as a guest, but instead of someone who'd come to her aid. And really the one person she knew she could turn to. "Do you want me to call him back?"

It was too late. Gareth was already in the kitchen rushing over to her. He obviously hadn't been up and ready yet as he was only wearing a pair of shorts, no shirt or shoes.

"Where is your maintenance room?" he asked.

Janet pointed. "It's the door across the room. I'm not sure what good that will do. We don't know what to do."

"Let me worry about that," Gareth replied.

"I'm sorry. I wasn't thinking when I called him," Brooke said to Janet as she watched him walk beneath the spraying pipes and disappear into the maintenance room.

"Like I said, Tabiq is full of surprises."

*Yes it is.* A few seconds later, the water began to ease up and finally slow to drips. Gareth came out and instead of walking back over to them, he climbed up on a counter and tapped one of the pipes. He shook his head and jumped down.

"Not good," he said.

"What's the matter?" Brooke asked.

"An issue I'll have to speak to Alex about. But the kitchen is not going to be functional for a while."

Janet's eyes widened. "You mean hours?"

"Days if you're lucky, but it could take weeks. I'll let Alex know what's going on."

"Would you care to fill me in?" Janet asked.

Gareth shook his head. "I'll leave that for Alex." Then he turned to Brooke and said, "Looks like you have to change. Want to walk back with me?"

Janet gave her a look then nodded. Brooke hadn't realized her white blouse was practically transparent since she'd gotten sprayed. "I think that's a good idea."

As soon as they were back in the hall, Gareth said, "I'm glad you called me."

"I feel horrible. It's not your job to rescue us."

"I wasn't rescuing anyone. I came because you asked me to."

Her heart skipped a beat. *He came for me.*

Nothing else needed to be said. Gareth took her hand in his and did as promised, walked her back to her room. When they arrived at her door he said, "I have a meeting today with Alex. I have a feeling it's going to go longer than I expected with this new development. Would you be interested in having a late dinner with me?"

"Gareth, I really want to say yes, but people are beginning to notice I'm not following the rules."

"You're not going to be fired."

She'd already figured that out, talking with Janet. "But it is not right that I can do what others can't."

"So have dinner with me in my room."

*Well there goes the rule entirely.* "Gareth, I want to, but . . ."

Gareth reached out and placed his hand under her chin, tipping it up so she couldn't avoid his gorgeous dark eyes. "Neither of us is going to be in Tabiq forever. Let's enjoy the time we have. I want to spend that time with you."

So much for her wanting to keep things private. Gareth leaned over and kissed her, and she didn't even try to resist. She'd expected that last night. This morning, it was unexpected, and even sweeter than she could've hoped for.

His lips lingered, kissing her gently. When he pulled away she found herself leaning against his bare chest, not wanting the moment to end.

"Dinner?" he asked.

"I . . . I can't go to your room. But I'll be here if you want . . . to have dinner in mine." Her room was far away from all the others, and the odds of anyone seeing them were slim.

He peered down at her and said, "I'll bring something for dinner. No need to order anything."

She wasn't thinking about food. All she needed was a few more of those sweet kisses and she'd be lost. "Let me guess, you're going to surprise me," she teased.

He pulled her closer against him. "You, my dear Brooke,

84

are the one full of surprises. And I'm starting to enjoy them very much."

He claimed her lips again, this time teasing and tracing her lips with the tip of his tongue. When he let her go, she was breathless and leaned against her door for support.

"I'll see you later for dinner."

*And I'll bring the dessert.*

She watched him strut down the hall, his body still glistening from the water. He was right. Neither of them were going to be in Tabiq for long. It was laid out on the table, no promises of tomorrow. How could she be disappointed when her knight in shining armor was so honest with her? She was getting what she wanted. Something real. *Just something not lasting.*

Gareth didn't want to be the one to deliver Alex the bad news, but facts were facts.

"You mean the pipe is rotted right through? How can that be? It's not like they've been there for twenty years," Alex stated.

"No. But the salt water and climate all come into play." *Never mind the shabby materials used.*

"This isn't good. And you think this could be a problem throughout the resort?"

Gareth replied, "I have no idea. If you want, I can have a team come and look into it. Was it all done by the same contractor?"

"No. So what you're saying is I need to call my brothers and deliver them this lovely news. Where should I start? That the resort might need some major repairs or that you're the one who found it?"

"I thought they knew I was here," Gareth stated.

"No. I monitor the guest list with Bennett. When I saw your name, I told him not to say anything to anyone. I'd handle it personally."

*No one handles me.* If Alex hadn't been so upfront and forthcoming, they might have gotten off on the wrong foot. "And this is where all our secrets start to bite us in the ass. I guess it's best not to mention my name. Brice was adamant that we not connect with any of you. He'll suspect that I came to Tabiq looking for answers he wouldn't provide."

"And he'd be correct."

"Yes, he would. Do you regret telling me?" Gareth asked. He knew Brice had similarities to Charles. As the oldest they felt the need to protect everyone. While all the others felt as though they were being controlled. It was nice to see that Alex didn't have an issue with being his own man.

"Only time will tell if I regret my decision. I guess it really depends on what you plan on doing with the information. Hopefully Ziva and I have explained what took place in Tabiq enough for you to recognize the ongoing need here."

"You have my word, the Lawson family wants all this to stop as much as the Hendersons. I'm sure if I spoke to my brothers, they would be more than happy to donate the steel required to make any necessary repairs to New Hope. It is important to continue bringing in industries that will strengthen the country."

"You haven't even told them what happened here, and you're that confident they'd be supporters to our cause?" Alex asked.

"This issue wasn't caused by just your father, Alex, and you know that. My family holds part of the blame. It is only fitting that this generation bands together to repair some of the damage." Repair might be too strong of a word. The best they could hope for was to make amends and try to stabilize the country enough so they weren't at risk for it happening again.

"So what you're saying is you'd like to be on the phone with me when I deliver this lovely news to Brice?"

It'd be better if done in person, but it wasn't like they had time to fly to Boston to address the pipe issues.

"Why don't we fix what we know is broken, and then you talk to your brothers when you're ready."

"And you're going to do what? Have the piping flown out here?" Alex asked.

"Why not? It'd save a hell of a lot of time if we handle the problem ourselves. Actually it might be the best way to address it right now. Just say the word, and I'll make the call."

"You're flying it from the States? Doesn't sound practical."

Gareth answered. "It wouldn't be, but a year ago we set up a steel mill just a few hours' flight from here. We're going global and needed to ensure quicker access to a quality product. Since we don't trust others, we set up our own plants. I'm sure you understand the trust issues we have. Sad when you find out you weren't just being paranoid. And things really are that fucked up."

"It definitely makes you keep your circle of people small. Not what I want for my children."

"Seems like your little girl is going to be just like her mother." Gareth said.

"Watch out world, because Ziva is a force to be reckoned with." Alex sat quietly for a moment and Gareth knew he was debating what to do. It all depended on whether Alex felt as though he could trust Gareth or not. Eventually Alex said, "Make the call."

"Okay. Do you need men to do the repairs or just the parts?" Gareth asked.

Alex shook his head. "We try to utilize as many people from Tabiq as we can. They can use the work, and they definitely need the money."

Gareth pulled out his phone and dialed the plant. There was no time to dick around so he went directly to the director of the facility. He placed the order and said, "This does not get keyed into the system. I will be paying for this delivery myself."

"I do not understand, Mr. Lawson. This isn't for a customer?"

"No. It's for my own personal use. And by the way, I need that delivered today."

"Yes sir. We'll have it transported to you immediately. Is there anything else, Mr. Lawson?"

Gareth wanted to say not to mention it to his brothers, but that would be like waving a flag of more suspicion. "No. That's all I need right now." He ended the call and slipped the phone back in his pocket. Turning to Alex, he said, "It'll be here. Now let's get this kitchen up and running."

Alex shook his head and said, "I never would've thought the Lawsons and Hendersons would be working on anything together, never mind here in Tabiq. If only our ancestors could see us now."

"They'd probably be rolling over in their grave thinking about how irresponsible we are with our money. I never thought I'd be so thrilled to be a disappointment before."

Alex laughed. "You and me both. Well, let's give some work to these good people and disappoint our grandparents even more."

When he and Alex arrived back at New Hope, they were

approached by someone whose hands were covered in grease and looked like he just crawled out from beneath a car.

"Hi, Alex. Janet called me and said there was a broken pipe. Do you want me to take a look?"

"Vinny. I was about to call you. How do you feel about giving us a hand again? We are going to use as many people from Tabiq as possible, but most likely you will know most of them from before," Alex stated.

"So it's not just a pipe?" Vinny asked. Alex shook his head. "Janet is horrible when it comes to describing what is broken. She always makes it seem better than what it really is."

"I wish she was right," Gareth said. "We're going to need all the pipes ripped out and replaced."

"I'm a mechanic by trade, but I've worked enough construction to make the place look pretty again afterward. How are you getting everything here that quickly? It's not like we have that much industrial material lying around here."

Alex answered, "I've got connections. I only need the hands to do the work. Glad I can count on you."

"Always. Besides, the longer the kitchen is down, the more stressed Janet will be. You know where that will trickle down to, right?" Vinny laughed. "They say, 'happy wife, happy life' for a reason."

Alex nodded. That was one thing Gareth couldn't relate to. "I'll take your word on that. Now what do you say we get inside and start ripping shit out." He still had a lot of pent-up frustration from that kiss earlier. A good physical workout would hopefully ease some of that tension. Just not in the way he'd like.

"You seem to be in a rush to get this done," Alex said. "Should I assume you have plans tonight?"

"I do. But don't worry, Alex, I'm not going to walk away

from this. You have my word." Gareth knew Alex had taken a huge step in trusting him, now he had to prove that wasn't a mistake.

"Good. Because the staff at New Hope needs you right now," Alex stated.

*And I'm the one Brooke called.*

# 7

Brooke wasn't surprised when she received the text message from Gareth needing to delay their dinner date. Everyone at the resort knew there was a major project going on in the kitchen. Somehow she knew Gareth was there, working with the others. It made sense. He was friends with Alex. And that is what friends do.

But that didn't mean she wasn't disappointed that they weren't having their night together. Gareth's time on the island seemed to be going by so quickly. If she wasn't careful he'd be gone and she wouldn't have seen him again. It really sucked, but what could she do? If she went to the kitchen, she'd only be in the way. She didn't know how to shut the water off, never mind fix the problem.

Sitting in her room waiting to hear from him wasn't her style either. If he was working, he was probably hungry. The other kitchen, the one they used for outdoor events, was still functional. She could easily slip inside and make him a sandwich and take him a cold drink. The longer she thought about it, the better the idea sounded.

So she slipped on her sandals and headed out to the event

kitchen. There was very limited staff on at night, mostly for room service orders. But she knew where most everything was. When she opened the fridge her first thought was make something simple, like peanut butter and jelly. But then she noticed lobster, grilled with garlic butter, sitting there like it was calling her name. Tabiq had the most amazing seafood and Gareth seemed to enjoy it.

*Might as well do it right.*

She cracked the shell and pulled out the sweet pieces of meat. Then she grabbed a large roll, sliced it and loaded it up with butter. Slapping in on the hot grill, she waited until it was toasty brown. Taking it off, she slathered it again with butter, which melted immediately. Then she carefully laid out each piece of lobster in the long roll. Brooke had to admit, it looked as good as when the chefs made it.

She placed it on the tray with a bottle of water and headed back toward the main kitchen. Once she was close she could hear the banging of tools. Brooke peered inside the doorway and right away Alex saw her.

"Be careful if you come inside," he called out. She looked around, still holding the tray, and stepped inside. Alex walked over and said, "That looks amazing. But I'm guessing you didn't bring it for me."

She hadn't planned that very well. How could she make something for Gareth and not think of the others? *Simple. I was only thinking of him.* "I'd be happy to go and make you one too."

"That's okay. Ziva delivered something for me to eat earlier. Guess you ladies think alike. Keep your men well fed."

*He's not my man.* "I figured he wouldn't stop to eat." She looked around but didn't see Gareth anywhere. "He doesn't seem to be here right now. Maybe someone else would like the sandwich."

"Don't you dare," Gareth's voice boomed from behind her. "I step out for one minute and you'd give my dinner away?"

She turned to him to defend her actions but was met by a huge grin and then a brief kiss on the lips. Brooke was so stunned she almost dropped the tray. Not great for someone who viewed themselves as a top-notch waitress. Quickly she steadied the tray, which was easier than steadying her nerves. What was Gareth thinking kissing her like that in front of Alex? And it wasn't just Alex either. There were other men working in the kitchen.

She looked around, but no one seemed fazed by the inter-action between them. That didn't mean it was right. Brooke handed him the tray and said, "I thought you might need something to eat."

He took the tray and asked, "Where is yours?"

"I only made one for you." *And that was one too many.*

"Come and sit with me. We can share this one," Gareth said as he ushered her to the side of the room where no one was working.

Once alone, she said, "I didn't come here to eat. Just to make sure you did."

He smiled. "Thank you, but I have a feeling you haven't eaten either, am I right?" She nodded reluctantly. He picked up the sandwich and tore it in half. "I cut, you choose."

"What?" She looked at him holding both pieces.

"Sorry. I forgot you are an only child. It's the only way we ever shared anything equally. One cut and the other got to pick first. So you never took more than your share."

"I would think with all the money the Lawson family has, there would be plenty to go around."

"There was, but my mother taught us it didn't matter how much you had. And by doing it this way, it'd always keep us honest."

She cocked her head. "Did it work?"

He held up the sandwiches and asked, "You tell me."

Brooke took a closer look at each half. "I think she taught you well." Then she graciously took the one on the left, leaving him the one on the right. "But I have no idea how you expect to split that bottle of water," she teased.

"That might be more difficult."

"Then I suggest you drink it. Since you've been working all day, you need to stay hydrated," Brooke stated.

"And you haven't worked?" he asked.

"Not like you have. Look at all this." She reached up and pulled some debris out of his hair. "You're really hands-on, aren't you?"

He nodded. "Feels good. Alex is too. I never would've thought he and I would be doing this together."

"Not the vacation you planned?"

He laughed. "Not even close. It's actually much better."

"Good. Maybe you could extend your stay and enjoy it a bit longer." She hoped that wasn't as obvious as it sounded.

"I'd like nothing more, but I have an obligation I can't get out of."

"Oh," she said softly. It was going to end very soon, whether she liked it or not. And she didn't.

Gareth added, "Trust me, I'd stay if I could, but my brother Dylan is getting married and I'm his best man."

That actually made her feel slightly better. It wasn't just another job or another place to be. Family was important to her, and she was glad to know it was to him as well. "I'm sure you're going to look fantastic in a tux."

"Funny, I have no idea what I'm supposed to wear."

Her eyes widened. "Are you serious?"

"Unfortunately, I am. I guess that is stuff women normally take care of, and if you haven't noticed, I'm single. Maybe I'll wear jeans."

She huffed. "Now I know you're joking. I can't believe I almost believed you."

"Sadly, part of that is true. Sofia, the woman he's marrying, wants something small. Her mother on the other hand, is going to want something—"

"Fancy?"

"No. Her parents own a restaurant. I'm guessing it's going to take place there. You'd think by now someone would've clued me in as to where to be. But don't worry. I can put together a bachelor party in a matter of minutes."

*Strippers. Ugh.* "Please, spare me the details."

"Hey, we know how to have a good time."

"I'm sure you do. But no woman wants to hear about it."

"Do you really think I'm going to hire strippers? I was actually thinking about flying out to Vegas and gambling. I mean, hell, he's getting married, how much more of a gamble can you take than that?"

"So you're not a fan of marriage?" she asked.

"I am. For other people. I can't picture myself settled down."

"But you're the one who was born and raised in New York. Sounds pretty settled to me," she teased.

He laughed. "You're right. Maybe I need to try your lifestyle for a while."

She handed him her dirty dish and napkin. "Here you go."

"What's this for?"

"My lifestyle." She got up and started toward the door but added, "I'm a waitress remember?"

She could hear him still laughing as the door closed

behind her. She really should've cleaned up and taken the tray back to the other kitchen, but she could do that in the morning. The look on his face was priceless. Brooke knew she'd hear from him tomorrow when things quieted down a bit. But tonight, it felt good getting in the last word. With Gareth, that wasn't an easy thing to do.


Gareth finished the last bite of the sandwich then set the tray on the vacant chair. He'd been tempted to chase after her, but his work was far from over tonight.

When he walked back over to Alex he said, "You don't have to stay if you have something else you'd like to be doing." *I sure as hell do.* "If we keep at this, the piping will be done tonight, and Vinny can come in with the crew and put it all back together."

"You know this isn't your issue. You've done plenty by getting the materials here so fast."

"I know, Alex, but if we're doing this, we might as well jump in with both feet."

"Are you sure you're not doing this so Brice doesn't flip out later?" Alex asked.

Gareth chuckled. "If you haven't noticed, I'm not quite the rule follower in my family either. So if I don't give a shit what my brothers are going to think about this, then I sure as hell don't care about what your brothers do."

"I bet you'd get along great with my kid brother, Dean. He's a lot like you. Or at least he was until he met Tessa, his wife. Funny what family will do to a man."

"Makes him weak?" he asked.

Alex shook his head. "Actually I think it has made all of us much stronger than we were before. Maybe not as fierce, which is also a good thing. But if it weren't for the women we have in our lives, I'm not sure what we are doing in Tabiq would be taking place. It's crazy, but they keep us . . . grounded, in a good way."

Gareth had noticed that with Charles and now saw the changes in Dylan. Before Rosslyn, Charles could only see things one way, his. Had marriage opened him up to listening to others? He wasn't sure. It wasn't that Charles gave in, but at least he let you finish what the hell you were trying to say. And Dylan, well he seemed to be enjoying home-cooked meals and being home at night. Neither change was bad, just . . . different.

"You seem to be getting along with Brooke. Is it . . . serious?" Alex asked.

That was none of his business. He wouldn't have answered his brothers if they asked. "I'm not the serious type." That was all Alex was getting, and actually the truth. But there was no doubt Brooke was the kind of woman who deserved someone more . . . steady. Yet she had said several times that she liked her no-ties lifestyle. He assumed that meant in relationships as well.

"Too bad. I don't know her very well, however Janet, Vinny's wife, speaks very highly of Brooke. But if you're not interested, I'm sure she will find someone who is."

Gareth might not want a serious relationship, but the thought of her with someone else didn't sit well with him either. "Oh there is no doubt she could do a hell of a lot better than me."

"That's exactly how I feel about Ziva. But for some reason, she loves me anyway. So what do you say we get back to work so I can get home to her before morning?"

"You do know you don't have to be here," Gareth said.

"Actually, I do. If anything goes wrong, this was my call. I don't want anyone else taking the blame. Besides, you never know when I'll need to know how to change a pipe in my own house." Then Alex laughed. "Yeah, Ziva won't ever let that happen."

"Doesn't trust you?" Gareth asked.

"She knows me too well. I have been known to lose my temper at things that break around the house. So now she makes me call a repairman. She said it's easier to fix it than replace it when I'm done."

"I wish you'd have told me that before you started to help. Should I double check your work?" Gareth joked.

"No. I didn't say I couldn't fix things. I said I don't have a lot of patience with things that break. Guess that's why I was great at ripping those fucking broken pipes out." Alex laughed.

"Great. Now comes the fun part. We put it all back together." If Gareth didn't believe Alex could do it, he'd have told him so. It didn't matter whose place it was, it needed to be done correctly.

They spent most of the night doing exactly that. But it was worth it. The guys Alex brought in were hard workers. Unfortunately not all of them spoke English. If there were questions, another interpreted for him. Surprisingly, this was one of the smoothest jobs he'd seen in a long time. The Tabiqian people sure as hell weren't lazy and were eager to prove their worth.

It was almost midnight when he realized he hadn't texted Brooke to thank her for dinner. He could do so now, but she probably was in bed. Her shift would start in a few hours, and if she was half as tired as he was, she was beat. His part of the repairs was complete, and tomorrow he would make it up to her.

*For a guy who said I'd never stand her up, I seem to do it a lot.* Valid excuses were still excuses.

"You saved my ass today, Gareth."

"No. I'd say Brooke did. She was the one who called me when no one else knew how to shut off the water."

"Brooke did that? Why is it I'm just finding that out now?" Alex asked.

"Probably because we had bigger issues to address."

Alex looked at him and asked, "Are you still planning on leaving in a few days?"

"I am. Dylan is getting married and—"

"Wow. I didn't know. It's kind of crazy that we're related but really know nothing about what is happening in each other's lives. And really, I'm not sure that's going to change."

"There's a risk if it gets out, you know. I'm not saying I agree with Brice, but he kept his mouth shut for a reason. It might be wise for us to keep doing so." Gareth was going to talk to his brothers, but he wasn't sure if he would include everything.

"Then I guess I'll keep your name out of the conversation when I talk to Brice tomorrow. Speaking of tomorrow, what are your plans?" Alex asked.

He'd leave now if it weren't for Brooke. He had only forty-eight hours left on the island and wanted to make every moment count. "Not that I don't enjoy spending time with you and your family, but I'm hoping to spend some time with Brooke before I go."

"I guess I owe her for her quick thinking this morning. What do you say I give her a couple days' vacation?"

"That'd be awesome," Gareth said.

"Don't get too excited. I didn't say she'd want to spend them with you," Alex joked.

Gareth snorted. "Good point. When are you going to tell her?"

"I'll have Janet text her first thing in the morning. Why?"

99

"You wouldn't happen to know of any place else besides New Hope on the island that is secure to stay at, would you?" Gareth asked.

"My mother runs a small inn. It's not fancy at all, and usually only the locals go there on special occasions. No pool or Jacuzzi, but what you get is a place on a hill with the view of the ocean."

"I didn't know your mother was here," Gareth said.

"She's Tabiqian. Yet another story for another time. Do you want me to message her tomorrow as well?"

"That'd be great. And, please don't tell Janet. I'd really like to surprise Brooke with this myself."

"You've got it. Now if you don't mind, I'm going home to sleep. One of us still has to work tomorrow." Alex extended a hand. "Gareth, if I don't see you again before you go, it was really nice getting to know you. Like I said, our door is always open and you're welcome any time."

"Thanks, Alex. If you find yourself in New York, give me a call."

Gareth headed up to his room to take a long hot shower. He was exhausted, but he knew sleep wasn't going to come easily. There was unfinished business, and he needed to resolve that. *I promise, tomorrow is all about you, Brooke.*

# 8

"What do you mean I have the day off? I'm scheduled all week," Brooke said.

"Mr. Henderson asked me to tell you to take the next few days off with pay. There was no explanation, not that he has to give one. He does own the resort, you know," Janet stated.

"Janet, I don't understand why." She hadn't asked for any time off. Brooke also didn't want special treatment. Everyone here worked hard.

"Maybe the question is why you don't want to take it. Mr. Lawson is only going to be here a few more days. I'd think you might want to spend some time with him."

"Is that what this is all about?" *Damn it, Gareth. Did you do this?* Not that it wasn't a really nice gesture, but she didn't want anyone manipulating her life. Not even if it was something she wanted.

"I really don't know what made him give you the time off. It's not my place to ask either. If you don't want to take it, I suggest you take it up with Mr. Henderson. Otherwise, consider yourself on vacation for a few days and enjoy. God knows I would," Janet sighed.

Brooke knew she was being foolish arguing over something like this. "Okay, Janet. I guess I'm on vacation for the next few days whether I like it or not. But if something changes, I'll probably be hanging by the pool or at the beach. I have to finish Alex's book."

"You're still reading it?"

"I've been busy," Brooke said.

"I don't care how much time you give me, that book is too . . ."

"I know, real. But I feel horrible not finishing it."

"Not as bad as you're going to feel without any sleep for the next few days," Janet teased. "There has to be something better to do than torture yourself."

That was horrible, but so true. "I'm sure I'll find something to do. I'll see you around."

"I hope not," Janet warned before she ended the call.

There wasn't much she could do with only a few days. It wasn't like she was going to fly back home for a visit. Most of the time would be spent on a plane. She'd rather be working than doing that. Besides, she'd be seeing her parents again in two months. A surprise visit actually would make them worry more than make them happy.

The one thing she knew she could do right now was strip out of her uniform and get comfortable. The thought of putting on her pajamas again and staying in bed all day was definitely appealing. This past week had been a rollercoaster. Either she was out late with Gareth or in her room unable to sleep because she was thinking of him. A couple days off might be exactly what she needed to rejuvenate.

*That and a hot cup of tea.*

There was no way she was calling down for room service, and if she showed up in the dining room now, it'd feel too weird. So how exactly was she supposed to enjoy this time off? *Trapped in my room and hungry. This is great.*

Brooke knew Alex meant well by giving her time off. But she liked to be active. Sitting in a room was boring. So she made up her mind. All those fun activities she'd been trying to get Gareth to do . . . she was going to do them. From scuba diving to fishing to parasailing. She might not be rested when she returned to work, but damn it, she was going to have some fun.

She quickly changed out of the uniform and into her shorts, T-shirt, and sandals. Then she rummaged through her suitcase to find her sunglasses and large wide-brimmed white hat. She peeked in the mirror and laughed. If she put these on, she'd look like she was auditioning for a role in an old classic movie. At least it was practical.

It was early, but the sun was already up. Most people would still be in bed or enjoying the indoor facilities. She didn't bother bringing a beach blanket because she just wanted to walk the shoreline and enjoy the waves breaking on her feet. An early morning dip was out of the question. She considered herself an average swimmer, but never would go out alone or without a lifeguard keeping an eye. Tabiq was known for having some strong rip currents. Brooke wasn't planning on starting or ending her vacation dead.

Sure enough, when she made it to the beach, it was deserted. Someone had left a towel lying there, but that wasn't uncommon since they belonged to the resort. The cleaning crew would be around soon and retrieve it. She was on vacation and going to try really hard not to work. As she began to walk by it, she couldn't resist. *Damn it.* She bent down, picked it up, and walked over to dispense it in the dirty linen bucket back by the gate.

That was it. No more. She wasn't going to clean the entire

beach. Focusing, she made a beeline for the shore. Brooke slipped off her sandals and let the ocean run over her feet. It felt so much warmer in the cool morning air. It actually was never cold in Tabiq, but the mornings were what she'd consider comfortable. It was the temperature that made you want to sit on a porch and drink raspberry iced tea and talk with friends.

Although she didn't want to admit it, she was beginning to miss home. She loved traveling all over the world, and was looking forward to the next adventure, but so much had happened while she was away.

Gareth's mention of his brother's wedding reminded Brooke of how many weddings she'd missed. No one bothered asking her to be a bridesmaid, as they all assumed she wouldn't be around. They were right. That didn't mean she didn't hate missing out, or being asked.

For the first time she hadn't planned her next job. What had caused her to delay? Maybe she needed to take a year off and regroup. Normally she only took a month between jobs and got all her visiting in then. An entire year might be too much. Not only would her parents get sick of her, but so would her friends. Three months might be her max. It'd also provide time to job hunt, since she'd been dragging her feet on doing that while in Tabiq.

She could blame the spotty internet service, but that would be a lie. The Hendersons were able to set this place up better than many big cities in the States. When she had asked about it, they said staying connected to loved ones was very important to them. That was good, because it seemed to benefit everyone in Tabiq too.

New Hope not only was a place for tourists to come and relax, but adjacent to it was a sports bar that was very popular with the locals. She'd gone in a few times, but it didn't matter what channel they had on, nothing held her interest. She remembered there were race cars going around and around and she asked one of the men what the score was. Brooke practically got thrown out of the room. That place was too . . . serious for her.

Another wave broke, this time higher, hitting her knees. She was daydreaming and hadn't noticed she was stepping into deeper water. It was so refreshing, and the feel of the salty breeze made her close her eyes again. If she wasn't standing, she might actually fall asleep. It was so . . . peaceful.

Since she worked the morning shift, she didn't normally have this opportunity. Off in a distance, Brooke could hear the cries of the seagulls as they searched for breakfast. Her own stomach growled, empty and wishing for something tasty. If she was lucky, they'd have a breakfast buffet set up outside when she returned. Normally it was in the main dining room, but that wasn't going to happen today.

It made sense now why Alex gave her a few days off. With one dining room down, they were overstaffed. Brooke would've been happy to alternate with someone else or float to another spot so someone else who might need or enjoy the time off could have it. Yet she wasn't in the position of making decisions. That's how she chose her jobs. You showed up, did your job, and then left without any stress.

But this past week had been stressful. It was like she had been on alert the entire time waiting for Gareth to pop up. He always knew how to find her, which was unnerving. But whenever she went looking for him, he was nowhere to be found.

She hadn't brought her cell phone with her, otherwise she'd try reaching out to him this morning. Most likely he was working with Alex again in the kitchen, and she really shouldn't disturb him there.

*Maybe that's why I got the time off. So I won't bother the workers.*

There was really only one she cared to see. And Gareth seemed to have enjoyed the dinner she'd prepared for him. Since she'd eaten the same thing, she knew she hadn't poisoned him. That was good. But she still wished she would've heard from him.

*When did I get so damn needy?* It was out of character. Miss independent didn't wait for the phone to ring. Half the time she would let it go to voicemail intentionally so the calls could be kept brief. And here she was hoping to hear from Gareth, and . . . nothing. The timing was off. She finally had all the time she needed to spend with him, and he was preoccupied with work.

Ironic. Was the universe laughing and toying with her? Getting her all interested, hot and bothered, then ending it before it could start? Maybe the cool breeze was what she needed to cool her desire for him. Yet the harder she tried not to think of him, the more she did. Even in this perfect setting, the one thing she'd change would be to spend time with him.

*This is ridiculous.* She wasn't a child. If she wanted to see him, she'd make it happen. The days of waiting for some man to call you or ask you out were over. Besides, he seemed very interested. It was a shame she'd already worn that sexy black dress for him. It would've been perfect to get his attention again.

Brooke turned and headed up the beach. It was time to take matters in her own hands. She was about halfway when she heard her name being called.

Turning back to the ocean, she saw one sexy Gareth rising from the water, carrying a snorkel in one hand and fins in the other. *Guess you're not working today.* She looked up to the sky and said, *Thank you.*

She waited for him to join her. When he did, she bit her bottom lip, as the water droplets dripped from his hair and ran down his chest. He definitely didn't have the body of someone who sat at a desk all day. Seeing him working last night seemed to have fit him better. With her eyes hidden behind the dark sunglasses, she soaked in all that perfection. Gareth's body glistened in the sun like some Greek god.

*Maybe a male model instead.*

A twinge of jealousy rose and she crossed that off the list. Although she was enjoying the view, she didn't want to share it with the rest of the world.

"I didn't expect to see you here," she said.

"And I thought you'd be sleeping late. Alex told me he gave you some time off."

She shouldn't be surprised she was the last one to know. "I'm not one who likes to spend the day in bed. Such a waste of a beautiful day. You never know what you'll miss when you're sleeping it away." *And look at the lovely sight I get to see.*

"I'm glad to hear that. Because I was hoping I could make up for my no-show last night."

"Gareth, it wasn't like you forgot. You were busting your butt helping out. I'm sure Alex appreciated everything you did for him." At least she hoped so.

"He did, but he doesn't require my assistance this morning. Vinny and the others will handle the rest. Which leaves me totally free for the next two days."

*Your last two days here.* It saddened her to think he was going so soon. "How do you plan on spending your time?" He stepped so close that the brim of her hat hit his chest. She reached up and pulled it off, but then the droplets from his hair landed on her T-shirt.

Gareth said in a husky voice, "With you. What do you say about a little excursion with me?"

"To where?"

"There is an inn on Tabiq that has a room available. Granted you can't walk the beach, but from the cliff you have a perfect view of the ocean."

"Gareth, you know we can't leave New Hope. I'll be fired for sure. Besides, we don't know if it is safe," Brooke exclaimed. She wanted to be with him, but not at the risk of their lives.

Gareth placed a finger under her chin and tipped her head up to meet his gaze. "It is safe. What do you say? Want to get out of here for a couple days?"

*With you, yes.* "It sounds good." A shiver of excitement ran through her.

Gareth looked around and said, "I'd offer you my towel, but it seems to have gone MIA."

She giggled. *And that's what I get for working when I shouldn't.*

"But maybe this will keep you warm for now." Gareth pulled her in shis arms and as one, their lips claimed each other's. Hunger built within her instantly. Gareth traced her lips with his tongue, and she opened to him. His body was still cool from the water, but as their kisses grew, she felt him warming to the touch. Gareth lifted her up in his arms, her feet dangling toward the sand. She dropped her hat and sandals and wrapped her arms around his neck. She couldn't get enough of him. She wanted it all.

A big gust of wind caused the sand to kick up, and she remembered they weren't behind closed doors. Painfully she felt him loosen his grip on her waist and slowly settle her back to the ground. Their lips were the last to part.

Panting, she said, "That . . . definitely . . . worked. If you . . . hadn't stop . . . I might have . . . overheated."

Gareth smiled down to her, "Then I suggest we go pack. I have a remedy for that problem."

*I'm sure you do.* Her heart was pounding and her mind was telling her this was foolish. All they were ever going to have was this one week. The clock was ticking with only two days left. Was she out to break her own heart? It sure would've been easier if Gareth had been working on the pipes today, but definitely not as much fun.

*Okay heart. Get ready for your high and then prepare for the crash.*


This was promising. Brooke seemed thrilled with the idea of a little getaway. And damn, that woman was passionate. Gareth couldn't wait to get her into bed, but he didn't want her to think that was all he was interested in. She was so much more than that. So he made sure the inn had a private candlelight dinner for two ready on the balcony where they could sit and talk.

He wanted to get to know her better. Although he actually knew more about her than any woman he'd dated. That was sad to admit, even to himself. Was he really so shallow that he never cared before what type of music they liked or what their favorite movie was? But those women didn't seem to mind. As long as they were wined and dined and well taken care of, they were happy. They were . . . relationships of convenience. Never thought about tomorrow, because most likely they weren't going to see each other again.

That was not how he thought of Brooke. He was looking forward to waking up to her in his arms. Crazy thoughts, coming from him. He hadn't slept with her yet, and he already didn't want to let her go. As they approached the inn, he began to wonder if it was a good idea. If he was feeling like this, he could only imagine what Brooke must be thinking. Gareth didn't want her to get the wrong impression. He wasn't looking for anything permanent. Yet he knew he wanted something with more sustenance, but he wasn't sure what that was exactly.

"You seem like you're a million miles away," Brooke said. "Are you worried about leaving New Hope and something going wrong?"

*Hardly.* "They have managed this long without me. I'm sure I'm not needed now." But it had felt good to be needed. Getting his hands dirty, back on the job like the old days, had felt right. "I guess I missed it."

"Missed what?" she asked.

"When I was in college, I took a summer off. I wanted to work on one of the construction sites as a laborer."

"You did? Why?"

"To get a better understanding of what they are faced with when installing the steel we manufacture. It was eye-opening."

"In what way?"

"Just about every way you can imagine. Right down to how we stack the beams, to what safety equipment we send along with them. I have to admit, part of me misses the physical hands-on part. A desk job was never for me."

"Then why do you do it?"

He laughed. "Because Lawson Steel has been around since 1808. It's a family-owned business, and it's my generation's turn to run it." There was a time when he would've said proud family, now he wasn't quite so proud. At least not about the past.

"I thought you had a bunch of brothers. Aren't they able to run it without you so you can do what you want to do?"

That seemed like such a simple question. One he'd thought about many times. He had tried not being heavily involved with what was going on at the office. All that did was make Charles drag him in harder. He'd never really had a conversation with any of them about leaving.

"You think it's that easy, do you? You haven't met my brothers. They aren't as easy-going as I am."

"Oh God help the world," she teased.

"Hey. What's that supposed to mean?"

With a soft giggle she replied, "I hadn't realized you were easy-going."

"For the record, I'm not. I'm an arrogant ass. On a scale of one to ten, I'm off the charts. I can make a person squirm with just one look. And—"

Brooke burst out laughing. "You had me squirming with just one kiss. But one look? Please, you're not scary at all."

"I'm glad you feel that way. Most people don't." He was worried she was going to call him a big teddy bear next. What were those sunglasses blocking out? Or did she choose to see what she wanted? Granted, he could be easy-going when he wanted to be, but in the world he lived in, if he was as soft as she made it sound, he'd have been walked all over. Even by his brothers.

"I guess you let me see a side that you keep from everyone else," she said.

That scared him more than being compared to a teddy bear. Mostly because she was right. He was different with her. But everything about Tabiq made things feel . . . different. That was something he needed to remind her.

"It's like being in another world over here. Nothing feels like it does back home."

Brooke nodded. "I know what you mean. You would think with everything these people have been through, they'd be full of hate and bitterness. Instead, they are overflowing with hope. Maybe that's what makes it seem different. Hope for a better tomorrow is contagious."

*And that translates to me being a sweet guy? I don't think so.* "I'm not sure, but I'm glad I came and saw it for myself. I never would've believed it otherwise. But as Alex and Ziva said, what they shared with us at dinner can never be shared with others." That had been meant for Brooke, not for Gareth. He knew almost everything that had already been said. He still didn't understand why Alex and Ziva would risk sharing that information in the first place.

*They trust her. And for some reason, so do I.*

"You don't have to worry; the secrets are safe with me. Even though I can't help now, I hope I can do something later."

He wasn't sure how she planned on doing that, but she was a hard worker. The Hendersons didn't need financial support, but they wouldn't turn it away either, no matter how small it might be. From what he'd learned about Brooke, she'd make it happen if she wanted to. "I'm sure they would appreciate anything you do. You know how to reach them when you're ready."

"Thanks to you. If you hadn't taken me with you to their home, I would still be ignorant to what New Hope is all about."

Brooke didn't know one-tenth of what New Hope represented to the Hendersons or why. But it was better that way. If she thought reading Alex's book gave her nightmares, the reality of what had happened in Tabiq would destroy her spirit. *That sparkle in her eyes would be no more.* He couldn't bear to think of that happening.

"Well, this is not the Henderson residence, but I hope you enjoy it anyway." They came to an inn that was more like a bed and breakfast. It definitely was a home. He could tell by the look on Brooke's face that she was pleased.

"This looks . . . inviting," she said, beaming brightly.

"Then let's go inside." Once inside they were greeted by a woman who didn't look at all like Alex, thankfully. "Hello. I'm Gareth Lawson and this is Brooke." He intentionally left off her last name. Not that he cared what the woman might think, but he cared what anyone thought about Brooke. "I believe you were expecting us."

She smiled. "My son told me some very special friends were coming to stay here for a few days. Welcome. My home is your home. Let me show you to your room."

When they entered, Gareth knew that Alex had redone her home; most things were modern on the inside, yet still very modest on the outside. That was wise. A woman such as herself living alone could easily become a victim to theft. But knowing Alex, she wasn't defenseless.

"You have a lovely home," Brooke said. "And our room is exquisite."

"I'm so glad you're pleased. Now go and freshen up. Your dinner will be awaiting you on the balcony. If you need anything at all, please ring the bell and I will come. Otherwise, I shall give you your privacy."

Once alone in the room, Gareth turned to Brooke. I'm glad you like the place."

Brooke stepped closer and whispered, "Do you know what I like about it most of all?" He shook his head. "I'm here with you."

Gareth wrapped an arm around her waist and said, "Are

you trying to distract me so we don't eat dinner again tonight? Because I've been trying to get this right from the first time I asked you."

Brooke said, "If I didn't think Alex would have our heads, I'd say let's start with dessert."

He could feel the blood pumping through his veins, and there was no way he could hide his desire for her. Resisting the urge to taste those sweet lips of hers, he said, "I promise never to invite you to dinner again."

She chuckled. "Sounds good. Now let's head to that balcony before we change our minds."

It wouldn't take much on his part, but Alex's mother had put a lot of effort into their meal and not eating would be very disrespectful. He wouldn't tolerate that treatment of his mother, and would never do it to someone else's.

*Damn. I am soft.*

When they arrived on the balcony, it was more than he'd asked for. Candles were lit everywhere, soft music played in the background, and the scent of fresh gardenias filled the night air.

"Oh Gareth, this is . . ." Brooke picked up one of the flowers and inhaled the scent. "I can't believe you did this."

*With a lot of help. A whole lot.* "I had a lot to make up for."

"No, you didn't. Actually I believe I cancelled on you as well."

He handed her a glass and said, "To new beginnings."

She took the glass and replied, "To new beginnings."

But when he took a sip, she didn't. "Is everything okay?"

Brooke nodded. "I don't drink."

Gareth smiled down at her. "I noticed that at the lounge. This is homemade ginger ale infused with fresh strawberries." It was one of the few requests he had made.

Her eyes watered, and he hoped that meant she was happy. Brooke raised her glass and said, "To thoughtfulness. May it never go out of style."

Gareth took another sip but he really wanted to taste it on her. "Let's eat before it gets cold." *And before I can't think any more.*

They spent the next hour actually enjoying not just the food, but getting to know each other better. It amazed him the places Brooke had traveled. She really was an adventurous one. But she wasn't wild or spontaneous. Each place had been carefully thought through. Just by listening to her, he knew she was brilliant.

"Your parents must be very proud of you," he said.

"I'd like to think so. They are loving and supportive of my choices, but proud, I'm not sure. I think they secretly hope someday I'll settle down and stay in one place. I'm sure you feel a similar vibe from your parents as well."

Gareth laughed. "My mother, yes. My father is a different story. He strictly thinks in terms of what would bring the company more success."

"That's horrible. There is so much more to life than money. If I wanted money, I'd stay home instead of living my dream."

"What would you be doing at home? An office job? I'm sure they pay more than a waitress makes."

"I'm not sure what I'd do. Actually I think I'd be bored silly. Imagine going to the same job every day for years. I couldn't do it." She huffed. "I know it sounds childish, but there is so much beauty in this world, and I want to see and learn all about it. Every place has its own culture, good and bad, but when I leave, I hope I have taken the best part if it back home with me."

"That explains why you're such an extraordinary

woman," Gareth said with sincerity. He noticed her cheeks pinken.

"Do you know you're the only person who can make me blush?"

He cocked a brow. "Really? Why is that?"

Brooke shook her head. "I wish I knew. I'm not sure if it's what you say, how you say it, or maybe . . ."

"How I make you feel?" he asked. She nodded. "Brooke, I hadn't talked to you about it when I made the arrangements."

"What are you worried about, Gareth? Everything has been perfect," she said, looking puzzled.

It really was. Never before had he enjoyed the company of a woman when it didn't involve sex. He'd done everything he could to make tonight special, but was it enough? Should he ask for a second room? Should he sleep on the floor? It was presumptuous of him to assume she wanted to share a bed with him. All the indications said yes, but . . .

"Gareth, is something wrong?" Brooke asked.

He reached over and stroked her hand with his. "You're right. Everything has been perfect." *I just don't want to screw it up.* "I know we have one room, but if you're not ready, changed your mind, or if I misread this, tell me. We don't have to do anything you don't want to."

Brooke smiled. "Gareth, I knew exactly what you were inviting me for. If I didn't want to, I wouldn't be here. Or have you forgotten, I'm the one who invited you to *my* room last night for dinner. Granted, it didn't work out, but tonight is a new night."

"Then what do you say we call it a night and finish this discussion upstairs?"

"I thought you'd never ask," Brooke said, leaning over to kiss him briefly.

*I don't want to love you. But damn, Brooke, you're making it difficult.*

Gareth's pulse raced, and his cock ached to break free from the confines of his jeans. He'd fought the urge to pull her into his arms all through dinner. Every part of her seemed to tease him: her eyes, her smile, and that damn cute laugh.

Never had he wanted anyone as much as he wanted Brooke. It actually had caused him physical pain to hold back. But he didn't care if it was an hour, a day, or a year, he'd respect her decision. Even though he wanted her, he also respected her.

But as they made their way back up the winding staircase, he wanted to scoop her up into his arms and carry her into the bedroom. He had only a sample of the passion living deep within her. *I want it all.* He wanted to submit to the overwhelming need building in him, but instead he guided her to their room.

When they entered, it was different than before. The fresh gardenias that were scattered all over the balcony were also in the bedroom, along with more candles. He couldn't have planned a more romantic setting if he'd tried. Although he wanted to see if she noticed, the hard bulge pressing against his zipper didn't care about flowers, or anything else. *I need to taste more than just those sweet lips of yours and I need to now.*

"Gareth, it's beautiful, but I . . . I . . ." Her lips opened, as her tongue darted out, and he felt like a man drowning. "There's nothing more beautiful than looking at you."

Did she know the torture she was putting him through? Did she ache for him like he did for her? *Fuck it!* There was one way to find out.

He moaned, knowing he couldn't hold back any longer. As his lips met hers, everything within him ignited. Brooke's hunger couldn't be denied as she met him with equal intensity. She opened to him, and his tongue eagerly tasted what she had to offer. Their tongues danced, sucking and nipping each other. Both gasping to catch their breath, neither willing to break their connection.

God, this was crazy. He couldn't get enough of her. Gareth wanted to tell her how beautiful she was, how good she felt and tasted. But the words wouldn't come as he was wrapped in a whirlwind of need.

Brooke's hand ran down his chest and rested on either side of the waist of his jeans, her fingers gently slipping inside. It wasn't raw passion or desire. It was letting him know it was okay, that this was what she wanted. Breaking their kiss, he looked into her eyes. The yearning was all he needed to erase any hesitation remaining within him. "I want you, Brooke," he muttered in a deep husky voice.

"I want you too, Gareth," she said softly, never breaking eye contact.

Gareth touched her cheek with the back of his hand, and she leaned into his touch. She didn't want it to stop either, which was good, because he couldn't imagine pulling away now. Gareth wanted to tell her all the reasons this was a bad idea. That they only had the here and now. That he'd be leaving for New York in two days. They might not see each other again. He couldn't offer what she deserved. But he couldn't bring himself to utter the words.

"If you're not totally sure about this, I suggest we stop now." Once he started this, he wasn't sure he'd be able to stop.

Brooke licked her lips while looking at his. "I'm not teasing, Gareth. I want you so bad that it hurts. Now kiss me already," she said breathlessly.

Claiming her lips, he parted them with his tongue. If he

thought his desire for her in that sexy black dress had been powerful, it didn't come close to what he felt now. It wasn't what she was wearing, but how bold and confident she was. He was giving, but she was taking. His tongue darted into her mouth and she sucked gently on it and then hers entered his, wanting the same. *Damn woman, you can kiss.*

The way she played with him with just her tongue, he could only imagine what that tongue would feel like stroking his cock. But as damn hot and horny as he was right now, his body couldn't handle her lips wrapped around him, licking and sucking. It would be over before he got started.

Tempting as it was, he resisted. Gareth needed to make sure she was taken care of before he was. If it took all night, he'd make sure she was satisfied, hopefully more than once. He wanted to do his own exploration with his mouth, but right now, they were both overdressed for it.

"I want to show you how beautiful you are."

As they stood by the full-sized bed, it felt tiny and cramped, but they didn't need more room, only less clothes. Their eyes never left each other as they quickly removed their clothes; shirts and pants flung in one direction, undergarments in another. Her bra landed on the lamp. He almost walked over and took it off, not wanting it to burn, but the fire between them was already roaring.

He looked at her breasts, full and perky, waiting for his attention. Gareth was eager to give it. He lifted Brooke into his arms and placed her in the center of the bed. Then he joined her, covering her body with his. Her taut pink nipples begged him to take them into his mouth. Lowering his head, he kissed, tugged, and nipped the first one. Her moans filled the air as she arched her back for more.

His tongue twirled around her nipple before he sucked

again. As she moaned, he moved to the next and continued his assault.

"Gareth, please . . ."

He ignored her pleas. Brooke reached up and tangled her fingers in his hair, trying to pull him up. He knew what she wanted, but she'd need to wait. He wasn't rushing this. Like dinner, he wanted this to be . . . perfect. More than perfect. He wanted it to be something neither would ever forget.

His mouth slowly made its way up from her breast to her neck, and then back down between her two perfect peaks. She groaned, tugging at him once again, this time more firmly. "Gareth, I want . . . I . . . need . . ." followed by an even deeper moan.

"Soon, sweetheart."

She was making it difficult to refuse her request. "Gareth, please." She gripped his arms, her nails digging into him.

He continued to flick with his tongue or nip with his teeth. His mouth inched lower, crossing over her abdomen as he continued his decent.

"Your body is so cool, until I touch it. And I'm going to touch you . . . everywhere," Gareth warned.

"Gareth," she moaned, arching against him.

"You feel so good in my arms."

"But I want to . . . feel you . . . taste . . . you," she moaned.

"Trust me. You'll have me, all of me." His words were muffled by her flesh. "But not until I have you first."

Brooke's moans echoed through the room, and he knew her need was building. Her hips wiggled, and she parted her legs trying to get them to wrap around his waist. "Please, I need . . ."

Gareth needed to address her need. He reached between her legs, his fingers finding her swollen clit. The instant he stroked her, he felt her shudder, and she opened farther for him.

He slowly circled it, bringing her higher.

"I . . . I . . . oh . . ." She responded softly in half moans.

Her body trembled as he repositioned himself, bringing his mouth only inches from her core. "You taste like heaven," he said, blowing on her intimately. An animalist growl echoed through the room, and she opened farther until he had full access.

Gareth slipped one finger inside her and pulled it back out. Then again and again. Brooke gripped the sheets as the building rhythm continued. His finger entered her again, and with his thumb he continued to circle her clit.

Now his own moans joined hers as he nipped her inner thigh and said, "I want to lick and suck you until you don't know your name."

She moaned, "Gareth."

He replaced his thumb with his lips, and she felt her body ignite and grow warmer. *Oh, yes.* His tongue darted out and licked again and again. He circled her clit, teasing her, then he sucked, enjoying the feel of her trembling legs as she was on the brink of losing control. He knew how to please a woman, but never had anyone been so responsive to his touch. It enhanced his need even more. She was so close to the edge, and he wanted to feel her explode around his fingers. Entering her deeply, he fingered her G-spot, stroking it firmly and quickly, while continuing to lick and suck her clit.

Her body went ridged, and her moans were almost whimpers of pleasure.

Gareth increased his onslaught and entered her faster and deeper with his finger until he felt her body jerk and her core clench around his fingers.

"Yes! Gareth. Oh, yes!"

As she lay panting, her body still reeling in the delights of her climax, he leaped from the bed, grabbed a foil pack from his wallet, and sheathed himself. Gareth returned to the bed, covering her body with his. Positioning himself between her legs, he lifted her hips toward him. The tip of his cock stroked her wet folds. As it touched her clit he watched her shudder again.

"Sweet Brooke, I need to be inside of you," he said.

"Oh, Gareth, I can't wait . . . any longer," she gasped then moaned.

His cock was so hard from holding back, it throbbed and ached. The look in her eyes sent him over the edge. It would be so easy to thrust deeply, but he didn't want to hurt her. Slowly he entered her, letting her get used to the feel of him.

She opened her legs, giving him access to enter deeper. Gareth's body demanded to move. He moved faster and deeper, his rhythm taking on a force of its own. "Oh God, you feel so fucking good."

"Yes. Harder . . ." she cried out. Brooke clung to him, her nails digging into his arms as her body shook, and the spasms of her orgasm gripped him like a vise.

*Fuck!* He couldn't hold back any longer. He continued to thrust into her as his body exploded into an orgasmic abyss. It was so powerful he could barely hold himself above her as his body trembled. *Fuck. Yes.*

There was nothing left, he couldn't hold himself up a moment longer and collapsed on top of her, his body tingling like never before. "What . . . the . . . hell . . . was that?"

Brooke replied, "I'll . . . tell . . . you . . . when . . . I . . . can . . . think."

He had never before lost himself in anyone like this. It

shouldn't surprise him that being with her was so . . . amazing. *Woman, what did you do to me?*

Although he didn't want to move, he rolled over, pulling her so she rested on top of him. He wrapped his arm around her waist so she couldn't leave.

Brooke nestled her head into his neck and said, "That was—"

"My words exactly," Gareth said and kissed the top of her head.

Brooke giggled. "I didn't say what it was."

"I know. There isn't a word to describe that, so don't bother trying." Kissing her head again, he closed his eyes. "What do you say we take a nap and wake up for a midnight snack?"

"Are you seriously thinking about food right now?"

"Who said I'm talking about food? Now sleep, before I change my mind," he teased.

She snuggled closer and said, "Be careful, I might be the one to wake you. You know, if I get hungry before you do."

*Woman, what are you doing to me?*

He tightened his hold on her. "Impossible. I have a growing appetite even now."

She giggled. "I'm sleeping already. Sweet dreams, Gareth."

What else could he have with this angel lying beside him? "Sweet dreams, Brooke."

He had no idea what tomorrow would bring, but today was absolutely perfect. If waking meant this was going to end, then he didn't want to wake again. *Because tonight, you're all mine.*

## 9

He would've stayed in bed all day, just so he could continue holding her in his arms. But Alex's mother had scheduled the time she'd serve breakfast on the balcony. Why had he agreed to all this?

*Because I wanted this to be something Brooke would never forget.*

Brooke stood by the railing sipping her tea, looking out over the ocean. She seemed to be a million miles away. Last night was beyond anything he could describe, but was she having regrets? There was nothing he could do if she was. It's not like he could go back in time and erase everything they had shared.

He waited another moment then couldn't stand it any longer. He needed to know what was troubling her. Getting up, his coffee cup in hand, he joined her by the rail. "It's a beautiful morning."

Brooke nodded. "And quiet. All I can hear are the waves crashing below on the cliff. This place is . . . magical."

"But?" Gareth never woke the next morning with the woman he'd spent the evening with. Spending the night would've implied something that wasn't there. But waking up with Brooke was what he'd longed for. Right now he couldn't read her expression to tell if she wanted that too. He held his breath, waiting for the bomb to drop.

"I didn't expect any of this Gareth."

"The—"

"Feelings," she blurted. "For the first time in my life, I'm standing someplace and thinking I could do this every morning for the rest of my life and never get tired of it." She turned to him, looked up, and added, "But Gareth, neither of us has that to give. You're leaving tomorrow night, and I'm going to be here completing my contract."

So she did want more. He knew that was a risk when he brought her here. It was like a fairy tale, but he was no Prince Charming. He planned most of this getaway, but what made it so pretty and elegant sure as hell hadn't been by his hands.

"It's difficult when the life you have and enjoy crosses paths with another, threatening to derail all you've wanted. But like the ocean below us, the waves come crashing in yet the cliff remains."

Brooke wrinkled her nose and asked, "Gareth, was this your attempt at poetry or deep philosophy? Because you're confusing the heck out of me."

"I guess I'm not good when it comes to this type of serious conversation." That was an understatement. He avoided them like the plague. He needed to get Brooke to understand, but more importantly, he wanted to make sure she was okay.

"So do me a favor and don't try to say what you *think* I want to hear. What I was trying to say was—"

The blaring of a horn echoed before the loud crash. Sounds of glass shattering and wood snapping filled the air as the entire house shook. Before he knew it, the balcony they were standing on began to give way, tilting slightly toward the water and rocks below. Brooke screamed and lost her footing. He saw her grip the railing, which no longer was secured to the house. Then another sound of cracking wood as the supports below the deck began letting go.

Another jolt; he felt helpless as her body fell forward. His heart stopped as the only barrier keeping her safe on the deck became a dangerous obstacle. Brooke's high-pitched screams were like knives piercing his heart. Everything moved so quickly, but his actions felt as though they were in slow motion.

Reaching out, he grabbed one of her hands, trying to pull her to him, but it was too late. Momentum lost to gravity. Her body swung over the broken railing and the only thing that prevented her from falling to her death was his iron-clad grip on her wrist.

If he wasn't careful, they were both going over. Gareth knew she was terrified, who wouldn't be dangling hundreds of feet off a cliff? This was no time to panic. He needed to let her know it was going to be okay while he tried to steady himself. There was no second chance to get this right. *Fuck!* This was really bad. "Hold on, sweetheart. I've got you!" Gareth said, trying to calm her, but his words might have been more for himself. No way was he opening his fingers, not for a second. If she went, he was going with her.

"Gareth. Help me. God, please help me . . ." Brooke cried out.

He was leaning backward to offset the angle as well as her weight. It was all about leverage, and he needed it to be in his favor. He looked around to find something secure to hold on to. There was a post to his left that appeared to remain anchored to the house. Arching as far back as he could, until his back felt like it couldn't bend any farther, he was able to reach it.

Yet in his new position, he could barely see Brooke. He knew he still had her. But they were running out of time. It wasn't like someone was going to stop and rescue them. This was up to him, and he needed her to trust him completely. "Brooke, can you reach up with your other hand and grab my wrist?"

"I . . . I don't . . . know," she whimpered.

In a firmer tone he said, "Brooke. Listen to me. You can do this." *You have to do this.* "I can't do it without you. Now reach up with your other hand."

He felt her wiggling, as she struggled, but eventually he felt her nails digging into his forearm. The most wonderful feeling. But it wasn't over.

"Gareth, what do I do now?" Brooke sobbed.

"I'm going to pull you up. No matter what, Brooke, don't let go. Don't look down. Just focus on me." He pulled slow and steady, with all his might. When she was finally back on the balcony and up against him, he reminded her again, "Don't let go." They were not out of danger. At any point this entire balcony could rip from the house.

"Gareth, what . . . happened?" she asked.

"I don't know. But right now, let's focus on getting off this thing. Do you think you can make it to the door if you crawl over me?"

"I . . . think so."

She did as he instructed, inching her way up as he held tight to her arm with one hand. "That's right. You're almost there," he said, never letting go of the corner post. Even as she made it to the door, he held on to her. "Okay. You're in. You're safe."

"But you're not. Gareth, pull yourself up before you fall."

Without her to worry about, he was able to swing himself into position and crawl up the ninety-degree-angled balcony. Once inside he pulled her into his arms. Gareth felt her shaking against him. "You're okay, Brooke. You're okay."

She ran her hand up his arm and then pulled away. Brooke held her hand up and he saw fear in her eyes again. "Gareth, you're bleeding?" He hadn't noticed he'd been injured. The adrenaline had taken over. "Let me look at it," she ordered.

He turned around and heard her gasp. "Oh my God. Gareth, your shoulder is . . . oh God. It's bad. Really bad."

He turned back to face her. "It'll be fine. I just need a bandage."

Brooke shook her head. "Gareth, you need stitches. A lot of them. We need to get you to the hospital."

"It's not that b-b-a-a-d . . ." He tried to fight it, but he felt himself swaying. "Br-ooke . . . I"

She hadn't known who to call but Janet. Thankfully Janet had been able to get help, but nothing had been close by, and minutes felt like hours as she kept direct pressure on his wound until help finally arrived.

Brooke hadn't spent any time at a hospital, not for herself or anyone she knew. This was an experience she'd be happy to do without. The doctors said Gareth would be okay. But until he was out of surgery and she saw for herself, they were only words.

She couldn't get the picture of his shoulder out of her mind. He'd lost a lot of blood. It wasn't just a gash, it was torn open, and a piece of wood had been stuck in it. She felt queasy again just thinking about it.

"Brooke, why don't you let the doctor look you over while we wait?" Ziva suggested.

"I'm not going anywhere," she replied firmly. "If it wasn't for Gareth, I'd be . . . well, I wouldn't be sitting here, that's for sure." No one knew how close she'd come to dying. But Gareth risked his life to save hers. He'd promised her she'd be okay. He said he wouldn't leave her, and she wasn't going to leave him.

"Alex told me what happened. What a place for that truck to lose its brakes and slam into the house like that. It actually pushed the house off its foundation."

"And us, almost off the cliff." If Gareth hadn't caught her when he had . . . *I'd be dead.*

"I can only imagine how frightening that was. And if Alex's mother had returned home, she might not have been so lucky. The front of the truck crushed the rocking chair she sits in all the time. It really is a miracle."

She could think of it as that, but there was a fatality, the driver of the truck. Brooke wondered if he had a family, a wife and children who were going to mourn his loss. Yes, it could've been worse, but Gareth was hurt and one man was dead. It didn't feel miraculous right now.

Brooke looked at her phone. Her mother was calling for the third time. They always spoke around this time of day, when she would've gotten off work and settling back into her room. Not answering it was going to cause unnecessary panic. Getting up, she said to Ziva, "Excuse me. I have to take this call."

Walking away also gave her a moment to breathe. Maybe talking to her mother about anything but the accident was exactly what she needed right now.

"Hello, Mother, how are you?"

"Brooke, I've been calling. You had me so worried. Is everything okay?"

She didn't want to lie, so she kept her answer vague. "Not the best day, but it could always be worse, as you say."

"I do. But sometimes, in that moment, it doesn't matter. Do you want to talk about it?"

"Not right now, Mother. I'm . . . tired. Why don't you cheer me up with one of your stories? What have you and Father been up to?"

Her mother laughed. "Your father has decided he wants to sell the house."

"What! Wait! What made him want to do that?" Not that she spent much time there, but when she was in the States, it was where she laid her head at night. It was the place she knew she could always return to.

"You're not going to believe this, but after all these years, your father wants to go home."

Brooke wasn't sure where that was, as they had moved so much. "To where?"

"Panama. He wants to slow down, relax, and spend time with family."

"I'm his family," Brooke said bluntly.

"You are. But you are not here, Brooke. This house is too big and empty. He wants to go and live near his papa and mama while they are still alive. You know, life is short, and no one is promised tomorrow. We don't want to spend all our time on the run. We want to enjoy the simple things now."

Brooke never thought about how short life could be until today. Normally she'd have accused her mother of trying to guilt her into staying home longer this time. But she wanted her parents to be happy and if her father had always wanted to return there, he should.

"Please tell me you're not moving before I return."

Brooke didn't want to think about where she was going to stay or what she was going to do. At least not right now. She already had enough stress worrying about Gareth.

"You know your father, when he decides something, he acts promptly."

*Great.* The timing sucked. Brooke was going to have to tell Janet she couldn't fulfill her one-year contract so she could go home and see her parents one more time before they sold their house and moved to Panama. She could always find an apartment somewhere, but why? It wasn't as though Brooke planned on staying there very long herself.

"Mother, I need to take care of a few things here. Maybe we can talk more about this tomorrow?"

"Of course, dear. But don't forget, you need to come home and get your things in order before we move."

"Yes Mother. I'll. . .I'll start making plans." Of course they weren't for the reasons her mother had hoped.

"Have I provided you a strong enough distraction yet?"

*Oh, not even close.* "You have given me plenty to think about. But Mother, I really need to go. I love you, and we will talk more about this later."

"I love you too, dear."

When Brooke ended the call, she turned back toward Ziva. The doctor had just come out and Brooke rushed over to him. "How is he? Can I see him?"

"He did well in surgery. We were able to remove all the wood and stitch him back together. It appears he also dislocated his shoulder. He must have been in excruciating pain."

*Holding on to me.* "But he's going to make a full recovery, right?"

"Yes. Did you notice if he hit his head? Because he appears to have a slight concussion."

*God, what else?* "I . . . I don't know. I wasn't able to see him from where I was." *Dangling over a cliff.*

Ziva said, "I wish Logan was here. He'd take care of him."

Brooke knew Logan was a top-notch neurosurgeon. *Please don't let him need one.*

The doctor didn't seem offended about Ziva wanting to bring in a specialist. If anything he seemed to be in agreement. "I wish he was here as well. Head injuries should always be monitored closely. But so should his shoulder and back. From what I hear you are the one who took care of him until he was able to be brought to the hospital."

"Yes. I did the only thing I knew." *That wasn't much.* Very basic first aid she had learned in high school.

"Your actions probably saved his life. It definitely saved his arm," the doctor explained. "But my recommendation is he gets home as soon as possible. He is not from Tabiq, and my fear is infection setting in. I cleaned the wound, but there are still particles inside."

She felt another wave of nausea. *Saved his arm.* She had known it was bad, but never had she thought he could've lost it. *Focus. Don't look back. Look forward.* Brooke nodded. "Get him home. Okay, I can do that," she said confidently, even though she had no idea how. She could ask her parents to use the private jet, but that would mean explaining everything to them. She could ask the Hendersons to fly him out as well, but that didn't seem like the right thing to do either. They were friends, but Gareth needed more. *He needs his family.* She would ask Gareth what he wanted when she saw him. "Thank you so much for taking care of him. Can I see him now?"

"He's still asleep. Why don't you give him another hour or two, then you can go in."

She nodded and the doctor left. Then she turned to Ziva. "You heard the doctor. We have to get him home. Do you know how to reach his family?"

Ziva shook her head. "Neither Alex nor I have ever met them. But I'm sure they are not that hard to find. Everyone knows of the Lawsons in New York. At least that is what Alex said. If you want, Alex can make the call."

"No. That's okay. I'll do it."

"Are you sure? You look like you're about to drop right here. I don't think you need the stress," Ziva said.

"Gareth talked to me several times about his brothers. I feel like I know them." Brooke never expected to meet or speak to any of them, but she knew this information needed to come from someone who truly cared about him, not from some hospital official or a Henderson, who she still wasn't sure if they were simply one of Gareth's customers. Even with everything she knew about Gareth, this showed her how little that really was. When they arrived at the hospital, she didn't know anything about allergies, medical history, or heck, even his date of birth. At least she could provide his family the facts, and give them the hospital contact information so they could call with any further questions. It was the best she could do for Gareth, and God knows she owed him.

"You promised you'd get yourself checked out once you knew he was okay," Ziva reminded her.

*But he's not okay, is he?* "I will. But only after I talk to his brother." She didn't need a doctor to tell her what was wrong with her. It was damage to her heart. Damage that was beyond repair. She almost lost the man she'd come to care very much about. *Everything has been perfect. Too perfect.*

"Do you want some privacy?" Ziva asked.

Brooke shook her head. Why? It wasn't like she was about to say anything Ziva didn't already know. Besides, it felt good to have some moral support. She pulled out her cell phone and searched for the number for Lawson Steel. Once she had it she hit call.

"Good morning, thank you for calling Lawson Steel, how may I direct your call?"

"Hello, I'm . . . I'm calling to speak to Dylan. Dylan Lawson."

"And who may I say is calling?" the woman asked.

"Brooke Cortes. A . . . ." She wasn't sure how to describe herself. "A friend of his brother Gareth."

"One moment please."

She listened to some classical music that did nothing to calm her nerves. When she heard the click, she took a deep breath.

"This is Dylan. You are?"

"Hello Mr. Lawson. I'm Brooke. And I am a . . . friend of Gareth's."

"The woman in Tabiq?" Dylan asked.

*Guess he knows more than I thought.* "Yes. There has been an accident. He's in the hospital. He just came out of surgery, but the doctor believes it's best he is flown back to the States right away to avoid any infection setting in."

"Fuck. What the hell happened?" Dylan barked.

Brooke could hear the concern in his voice. She proceeded to tell him exactly what had transpired. At least from the point when the truck hit the house. "The doctor is optimistic, but it is very bad. The doctor said it was a close call that he didn't lose his arm."

"It sounds like he almost lost a lot more than that. He shouldn't have fucking gone to Tabiq in the first place. Nothing is worth what just happened to him."

It was like a slap in the face, because his injury happened saving her. "I'm very sorry this happened to your brother. But

I'm sure he will be okay. May I give you the contact information for the doctor so you can make arrangements to transport him home?"

"Yeah. And I can have a jet there in a few hours. He's getting the fuck out of there. I knew nothing good was going to come from him being there. He should've left days ago when I told him to. But he wouldn't listen, and I have a feeling it has to do with you. If he had listened to me, he wouldn't be in this condition."

*God. Is Dylan right? Did he stay because of me? If I would've said no, would he be okay now?*

Her hands trembled and she said, "You'll have him back home soon. I'm sure they will take good care of him until you do."

Dylan said, "Thank you for calling and letting me know."

"I wish it wasn't to deliver such news."

She ended the call and the phone dropped from her hands. Tears streamed down her cheeks, and Ziva pulled her into her arms.

"It's okay, Brooke. You did the right thing calling."

"But he . . . he said . . . Gareth coming here was . . . all a . . . mistake."

"He's angry that his brother is hurt. His words weren't meant for you. If anything, it was meant for my husband."

Brooke looked up. "I thought they got along?"

Ziva smiled. "It's amazing what one can overcome when they choose to. And trust me, Brooke, this too will pass. Soon Gareth will be up and back to his normal self and you two will have a story to tell your grandchildren."

If that was Ziva's way of making her feel better, it wasn't working. This was all she and Gareth had. He was going home to his family and so was she.

"Thanks, Ziva. I should be talking to Janet about this, but I would like to cut my contract short, if that would be okay."

"With everything that has happened, it doesn't surprise me one bit." Ziva gave her a quick hug. "But you do know you're welcome back anytime. Work or vacation or just for a visit. Don't forget that, Brooke."

"I won't. Now if you don't mind, I'm going to sit with Gareth. Even though he's asleep, I just . . ."

"Want to be with him. And you should be. It's where you belong."

*Until the Lawson family arrives and I'm . . . what put their brother in the hospital.*

Gareth felt the stabbing pain on his left side and back. *What the fuck happened?* His mind was so foggy. He could remember screams. Whose were they? His? No. They didn't sound like his voice. Thinking harder. A woman. She was screaming for him to help her. He couldn't. She was . . . scared.

His heart raced, and he turned his head, trying to find her, but all was dark. *Where are you?* No answer. *Please tell me so I can help you.* Still nothing. The more he struggled, the more confined he felt. Something was holding him down. Why were they preventing him from getting to her?

*Tell me where you are. I'll come to you. Just call out to me again.* She needed him. He promised he'd be there.

The voices started again.

"His fever is still going up. Call the doctor."

*I don't need a doctor. I need to help her.*

"Also check his restraints. He was pulling out his IV again."

*Let me go.* He tried to move again and the pain shot through his body.

Once again he heard her. "Gareth. Don't leave me. You promised you wouldn't leave me. You have to fight. You're strong. I know you are. Fight for your family. Fight for me. Just . . . keep fighting."

He was trying, but no one seemed to be able to hear him. No matter how much he tried, they all spoke as though he wasn't there. All except her. Who was she? Why was he fighting for her? What was he fighting?

Gareth willed his eyes to open. They were heavy, so heavy. Just once, because he needed to see her. Pushing past the pain, his eyes opened, just a sliver. Everything was blurred and something was so bright it hurt his eyes. But then there was a shadow, a gentle touch on his hand.

"Nurse. He's . . . he's awake. Gareth's awake."

He tried to speak but only choked. Something was in his mouth.

She spoke to him again. "Please, Gareth. Remember your promise. You won't let go of me. So fight. You can fight this. I know you can. Trust . . . me . . . trust me . . ."

The voice once again sounded so far away. His eyes closed again; the darkness that was once there returned.

*I'll fight. I'll find you. I promise.*

Brooke ran out of the hospital room crying. Half of her filled with joy that Gareth opened his eyes, the other half saddened that the medical team asked her to leave so they could put him back in his medically induced coma.

They said it was what was best for him so his body could fight a staph infection. She wasn't in the medical field and no one was giving her much information. It was only what she overheard.

Brooke wasn't family, and as soon as Gareth was loaded

onto the medical evac jet, she probably wouldn't know what was going on at all. It was slowly killing her to know that in a matter of a few hours, she wouldn't see him again.

When she walked into the hallway, she saw Janet sitting there. "I thought you might like some tea and something to eat."

"I'm fine," she said.

"No you're not. You won't be any good to him if you don't take care of yourself," Janet explained.

"I'm no good to him now. Look at him. He has tubes coming out of his nose and mouth. He is strapped down so he doesn't pull out his IV, or any other tubes, again. And what can I do? Nothing but stand there and hold his hand."

"That might be all he needs right now. You'd be surprised how comforting that can be."

"I can't help but think that this is all my fault."

"Brooke, you didn't drive that truck into the house. And the man who did, had lost control of it. Nothing about this is your fault. It was just an accident. A very horrible accident."

"But he took me there because he thought he owed me. He didn't. I would've been just as happy at New Hope, where this wouldn't have happened."

"Gareth doesn't seem like a man who does anything he doesn't want to do. He brought you to that inn because he wanted to share something special with you. Hold on to that and let it be your strength through this. I'm sure, even though he's in a coma, he's holding on to it as well."

*I sure hope so.* "You do know he's leaving soon. They are flying him back to the States. His brother is going to accompany him."

"Why don't you ask if you can go too?" Janet suggested.

She shook her head. The last time she spoke to Dylan, she felt guilty, as though she was the one who put Gareth in the hospital. Deep down inside she knew that wasn't the truth, but she wasn't ready to see Dylan right now. How could she defend herself from what she didn't understand? Why was Dylan so angry that Gareth wanted to stay in Tabiq?

"It's not my place, Janet. Besides, I'm leaving too."

"I know. Ziva told me. You're going to be missed here."

"No one even knows my name," Brooke stated. Right now she didn't care.

"That is what you believe. The Tabiqian people keep to themselves, but that doesn't mean they don't care. It is a form of protection. Yet when they learned of your accident, many came to me to see if there was anything they could do for you."

She smiled. "Please tell them thank you. And I'm glad you told me. I'm going to miss New Hope very much. But with everything going on, I need to be home." She didn't bother telling Janet or anyone else what her mother had said.

"As you requested, your belongings have been packed and you have a ticket for the plane leaving tonight." Janet handed her the ticket. "But if you change your mind, you're welcome to stay."

"I know. But I won't." Gareth wasn't the only one who had some healing to do. Saying goodbye to him, especially in this condition, was like a knife to her heart. "I better get back inside. I don't have much time with him before they move him." She turned to walk back to Gareth's hospital room but stopped. She turned back again and rushed over to Janet. Giving her a tight squeeze, she said, "Thank you for everything. You've been a good friend to me while I've been here."

"And I hope we stay friends for a long time," Janet said.

Brooke sniffed back the tears that once again threatened to flow. She'd cried so much in the last few hours that there shouldn't be any left. But there seemed to be an endless supply.

When she walked back into the hospital room, the doctor was there. She expected him to ask her to leave, but he didn't. Brooke sat quietly in the chair watching and listening to everything they did. She had to admit, they were giving Gareth the best care they could here. But she was happy he was leaving. Logan had done some amazing things setting up this hospital, and the staff was spot on. But even back home, a staph infection was serious. That on top of the injuries and loss of blood scared her. This couldn't be the last time she was going to see him. *It can't be.*

She didn't want to be in the way as they prepared him to travel. She looked at the clock and knew Dylan would be arriving any time. She didn't want to be here when he showed up. His last words still stung.

Getting up, she walked over and softly asked the doctor, "Would it be okay if I spoke to him once more before I leave?"

He stepped out of the way. "Of course. I'm a believer that some people can still hear when they are sedated."

Brooke smiled at him. *I really hope that's true.* She stepped to the side of the bed and, once again, placed her hand inside his limp one. "Gareth, it's me, Brooke. They are going to be taking you home now. Dylan is almost here. I know you'll be okay." She leaned over and whispered in his ear. "I'll never forget you. You'll always be in my heart." *I love you.*

It was the first time she'd ever said those words to a man, and she hadn't even been able to utter them out loud. Brooke gave his hand a gentle squeeze before placing a kiss on his forehead. She didn't want to leave him like that. It felt as though she was abandoning him, and she'd promised to be there. She had thought for sure he'd wake up and everything would be okay. But it wasn't. And she needed to step aside.

There was no doubt he'd have all the love and support he needed back with his family. It just wouldn't be hers.

Brooke stepped away from the bed, her hand trembling. "Thank you for everything you did for him."

"I only work to heal the body. You were here for his spirit. Do not discredit how valuable you have been in his recovery."

*Recovery?* That was a word of hope. She wasn't going to let it go. Giving him a quick nod, Brooke left the hospital room for the last time. Each step was like a piece of her heart breaking. There was nothing she could do to change it.

As she walked through the main doors, she saw a black SUV pull up and a man jump out. There was no doubt in her mind it was Dylan. As he stormed past her, it was as though he never saw her there. It saved her the trouble of introducing herself and confirmed her decision to leave.

Brooke walked across the parking lot and got into the vehicle Janet had waiting for her with her belongings. She was leaving Tabiq. Leaving Gareth. *Leaving a piece of myself.*

---

If one more person asked Gareth if he needed anything or how he was feeling, he was going to knock them on their ass. The doctor gave him the all clear, all he needed to do was some physical therapy to work the muscles in his back and he'd be good as new.

Maybe not exactly like new, but not the broken man he was a few weeks ago. He never thought a dumb infection would be what almost took him out.

Maria walked over to him and said, "Do you have the rings?"

"I do." He patted his breast pocket to confirm.

"And your boutonnière. Where is your boutonnière?"

He couldn't bring himself to wear it or admit why. The gardenia was always going to remind him of Brooke. "I'm allergic to it."

"You are? You're not sneezing," Maria stated.

"No. Makes me feel tight in the chest." *Because the one person I could picture myself with walked away when I needed her most.* When he woke from the coma to find she was gone, it hurt more than the recovery process. He'd been tempted to call her, but what was the point? The scars on his back would only act as a constant reminder of probably one of the most horrific times of her life. If that was what she needed so she could be happy, he wouldn't try to stop her.

Maria said, "This is your brother's wedding. Look happy."

It wasn't a suggestion. He forced a smile and said, "This is my happy face. Count yourself lucky that Dylan is marrying your daughter instead of mine."

Maria scurried off muttering something in Italian. *That was easy.* If only the rest of the night could be so easy. Part of him wished Dylan and Sofia had kept their original wedding date. But Dylan wasn't hearing it. He insisted they would only get married once Gareth was well enough to act as best man.

He was happy for them, but all this talk of love and their future and children was more than he could handle right now. The doctors said it could take time to sort things out. That sometimes when you wake from a coma, your emotions are off. You have a hard time telling what is real from what was part of your thoughts while you were under. But his gut told him she was there, calling his name, telling him to be strong and to fight. At the same time, that same voice promised him she would be there. *And Brooke isn't here.*

This was merely one night to get through, then he could go back to his apartment, the place where he seemed to spend most of his time lately. The last time he'd been out for what was supposed to be fun had been the sad excuse for a bachelor party. It had been an utter failure. Instead of Vegas like he'd wanted, they all sat around talking about the Hendersons and Tabiq. What part didn't they get? He'd told them what he'd learned from Alex, nothing held back, at least nothing that was any of their business. Brooke was off limits, not that they'd asked.

Sofia's parents had closed their restaurant and turned it into a wedding venue. It wasn't the large wedding Maria had wanted for her daughter, but it was what Sofia and Dylan asked for. Just family and close friends. With everything that had gone on over the past month, it still was more than he wanted to see. But there was no getting out of it. The music started, the cue for everyone to take their seats. All except Gareth and Charlene, Sofia's best friend.

As they stood on each side of the floral arbor, Gareth closed his eyes. Dylan walked down the makeshift aisle and leaned over, "Are you okay?"

Gareth nodded. "Just listening to the music."

Dylan shook his head. "If classical is your thing now, I better talk to that doctor for you."

*Keep the mood light. Keep it happy.* It was the best gift he could give Dylan.

Dylan took his spot and turned around. The music changed and Sofia appeared, dressed in her white gown and holding on to Filippo's arm. She looked beautiful. As she walked down the aisle, it was as though no one was in the room except Dylan, as it should be. This was their moment, and no one in the room could doubt their love.

Gareth stood and only half listened to what the judge was saying. But when it came to their vows, Gareth shuddered.

Dylan said, "I promise to always be there. Trust me, if you fall, just take my hand, and I'll catch you."

*Take my hand. Trust me. I've got you.* He could hear Brooke cry out, feel her fear, but she'd trusted him.

*Help me. I need you.* The voices said again. But the question was always the same: Where was she?

Gareth couldn't concentrate on their union, as he couldn't

145

stop thinking about Brooke. Was she okay? Had she moved on to her next job like she had wanted? Did her near-death experience leave her rattled? Was it affecting her life, like it was his?

Gareth wasn't living in fear, but it had changed him. He used to live for the moment. Actually he remembered telling Brooke to do the same thing. His life had been full, and he'd been happy. But now he felt as though he was missing something, and that something was her.

Sofia had asked him if there was anyone he wanted to bring to the wedding. The only person he'd have even considered bringing to a family function was Brooke. But the last thing he wanted for her was his family asking a bunch of questions about the accident, and they would because he wouldn't answer them. He told them the only thing that was important, it was only an accident, no one had intentionally, tried to kill him or Brooke. That had been a very real concern of his. That his digging into Tabiq, somehow had put Brooke in danger. Risking his life had been one thing, one he'd do again if he'd still gotten the result he did. But he'd never wanted Brooke to be caught up in any of that shit. Thankfully it really had been nothing more than faulty brake lines.

But people wanted to know exactly how he'd been hurt? Hell, he wasn't exactly sure himself. He could only assume that when he held on to the post and pulled Brooke up, he'd been so worried about saving her, that he never noticed the splintered wood digging into his shoulder. He was lucky. It could've been much worst. *We might not have made it.* Even now, when he closed his eyes, he could see the fear on her face. Hear her plead with him not to let her go. If he struggled with the nightmares, he could only imagine what she was going through. He wanted to believe it was over for her. And if it was, Gareth wasn't going to be the one to bring it all back.

*It's bad enough one of us lives with it.*

"You may now kiss your bride," the judge announced.

Gareth had somehow missed most of the wedding. The only positive was he knew Dylan wouldn't be any the wiser. The happy couple walked back down the aisle, but midway Dylan bent down and scooped Sofia up into his arms.

"Time to rest those feet, Mrs. Lawson," Dylan said.

Sofia chuckled. "Whatever you say, Mr. Lawson."

The two of them headed to the back of the restaurant where a long table was set up to celebrate the joyous occasion. Charles walked over to Gareth and said, "You seem a bit . . . distracted. Anything you want to talk about?"

"Nope," he said dryly.

"You haven't been yourself since you got home."

"Tabiq was eye-opening. I guess it has changed me," Gareth replied.

"And what about this woman I heard about?"

"It's nothing." *At least it wasn't any more.*

"Is that how she feels or just you?" Charles asked.

*Does it matter?* "Charles, unless you haven't noticed, we're at a wedding. Let's talk about something else."

"If she means something to you, this is the perfect time to discuss it. Or didn't you listen to anything they said when they exchanged vows?" Charles asked. "Maybe I don't want to know that answer. But I think you have some soul-searching to do."

"I'm not doing that. But then again, I think we all have some to do. That meeting with Alex opened my eyes, Charles. We have been pointing fingers at others for how fucked up they were. We should've been looking in our own closets. Now we have some serious decision-making to do."

"We all know you well enough to know when you're planning something but haven't told anyone about it. Please tell me you're not going back to Tabiq," Charles said.

"And if I was?" Gareth asked. He didn't need anyone's approval.

"You haven't finished healing from the last trip. One that I wish you would've discussed with me first."

"So you could've told me no?" Gareth snarled.

Charles said, "Before Rosslyn, that's exactly what I would've done. But like you, I've changed. I'm not out to stop you from doing what you want. But I would've offered support. You do know we're still your brothers. You don't have to go do this on your own."

"I already learned everything I need to know about the Hendersons," Gareth snapped.

"I'm not talking about our cousins, and I'm not talking about Tabiq either. I'm not sure if it is the accident or if it is that woman Brooke, but whatever it is, we're here for you."

"Charles, I appreciate what you're trying to do, but there are some things I have to do alone." Figuring out his feelings for Brooke, determining what he wanted for his future, were at the top of that list.

"Well, I'm here if you ever change your mind. So are the others. With everything we've learned lately, it's more important than ever for us to stand together."

"Don't worry, Charles, my days of running amuck are over. Granted, I'm never going to be as old and boring as you are, but I'm settling down." *Not by choice.*

Charles laughed. "Gareth, one thing I know is you'll never be boring. There is trouble right around the corner, and it has your name on it."

Gareth laughed. "So what you're saying is I should spice up this party with one of my memorable toasts?"

Charles shrugged. "You can. But if you think therapy was hard for your shoulder, wait until you see what Maria could do to you. She's very protective of her kids."

"Hey, why don't you have Rosslyn go play matchmaker with Sal and Charlene. That's a couple that would be very entertaining to be around."

"What makes you think my wife is a matchmaker?"

Gareth shot Charles a look. "Because they all are. It's like some secret group, and they are always scoping out who should be with who."

"Then I guess Sal and Charlene are out, because Rosslyn said Charlene would be good for Seth."

Gareth almost choked. "Seth? She would eat him alive. He's never dated anyone like her. She's . . . bold."

"That's one way of putting it."

"I'm glad she didn't say my name," Gareth said.

"Nope. She said you're already in love. Just too dumb to know it." Gareth shot him a warning look and Charles added, "Rosslyn's words, not mine."

Rosslyn fit very nicely into the family. He could almost picture her saying that to Charles.

*Good for you, Charles. You found someone who can tolerate your arrogant ass.* He thought he had as well.

*Good thing I don't do relationships, or losing her would really suck.*

Gareth was glad Charles had come over to talk. He'd been on the fence about what to do, and now he knew. He needed to go back to Tabiq. There was unfinished business there. But letting Charles know would have to wait until tomorrow. Gareth had already distanced himself enough from Dylan's wedding. He wasn't about to blow the rest off.

"What do you say we head over there so I can give my toast before Charlene does hers."

"Are you worrying about hers topping yours?"

"No. But once she starts talking, it never ends. I figured I'd get mine in before they leave for their honeymoon." Gareth laughed. It was a good note to end the conversation with. *One that does not have the focus on me.*


Brooke was home and packed, but she knew she couldn't follow her parents to Panama. Like always, she'd visit, but that was it. To her father it was going home, but for her, Panama was only a vague memory.

So she did something she'd never done before, taken on a job without thoroughly researching every aspect. It had the similar feel to New Hope, just different people and a different location.

It didn't take her long to realize the driving force behind the place. Money. There wasn't any respect for the staff, and respect for the guests only took place face to face. Behind their backs, they slammed them all. It was a gossip fest, and she was sickened by it all.

After working there for one week, Brooke was forced to quit. She couldn't work with people like that. So she moved on to another place. It was better, but not by much. She couldn't stay there either. At the rate she was leaving jobs, she'd be lucky if anyone would hire her. Her spotless résumé was going to look like it had the chickenpox.

Brooke always had a place. If she wanted, she could check into a hotel and stay there until she figured things out. But she knew the issue. Nothing felt right because of how she'd left things in Tabiq. She needed to go back and face her demons. Or at least finish her contract.

Picking up the phone, she dialed Janet's number. Of course Janet wasn't the one who'd be able to make the final decision, but Janet could give her an idea of what to expect when she decided to call Alex.

"Brooke, I was hoping I'd hear from you. How have you been?" Janet asked.

"Good. But I still feel awful about not completing my assignment. What do you think Alex would say if I offered to come back?" That sounded a bit arrogant as though she was important. So she corrected herself. "I mean asked if he'd take me back. I'm sure he's already filled that spot, but maybe something else opened."

"You're right, the position was filled a few days after you left. There aren't any openings as far as I know, but then again, I'm not the big boss. I would say give him a call. The worst that happens is he says no."

That was exactly what she was afraid of. It'd be so much easier calling Ziva, but she had to follow the rules. Alex was a part owner with his brothers. Although she knew if Ziva asked, he never would refuse her.

"I can give him a call next."

"You might want to wait a few days. There is a big family reunion or something happening here right now. All the Hendersons are here with their families."

That was definitely not something she wanted to interrupt. When she was there a month ago, she didn't recall hearing anything about that. For all the Hendersons to be there, it had to be a big event. She normally wasn't such a curious person, but she asked anyway.

"Do you know why they are all there?"

"Nicolas, Brice's oldest is turning ten tomorrow. They are all here to celebrate. I would've thought it was easier for Ziva and Alex to travel back to the States, but what do I know? The Hendersons all do things differently than most."

If she hadn't left, she'd be there right now, probably

serving the entire family. Brooke had met many of them when they traveled to Tabiq, but they normally didn't bring their children. She had no idea why she was becoming fond of them, but she was.

"I bet Charisa is loving it. She finally will have kids to play dollies with." That didn't mean Charisa would let Brooke off the hook next time.

"So where are you now?" Janet asked.

"I'm . . . going home for a few days. Then if things work out, Tabiq will be my next stop."

"If it doesn't, I have a friend who works on a cruise line. I could always call and get you a job there."

That was really nice of Janet, but it wasn't a financial issue. She wanted to continue her dream of traveling the world.

*Then why am I going back to someplace I've already seen?*

That had nothing to do with finishing a job. She felt lost, and she hoped by going back, maybe she wouldn't feel that way any longer.

"Thanks, but that isn't what I'm looking for, Janet. If Alex doesn't need me, I have a few other places in mind."

"Okay. Hey have you heard from Gareth? I was wondering how he is doing."

Brooke wasn't going to admit it, but she was following him in the media. There had been a photo of all six Lawson men standing together at Dylan's wedding. From what she could tell, he looked like he was happy and back to his old life.

"I haven't spoken to him, but I hear he's doing well."

"You mean you haven't called him?" Janet asked.

"No. He had a lot going on, remember?"

"Had. But that was over a month ago. The last I heard,

they were able to clear up the infection. Thank God. I was really concerned the last time I saw him. It . . . didn't look good."

*No. It didn't.* "He's a fighter."

"But that doesn't answer why you didn't call him. It seemed like you two were really getting along. I would've bet that you ended up as a couple."

"And you would've lost that bet. Our lifestyles don't mesh with the word couple. And long distance relationships aren't for me before you even suggest that." Brooke knew Janet was a hopeless romantic now since Vinny had swept her off her feet. But that fairy tale didn't happen to everyone.

"Okay, so you're not going to live happily ever after. But you can still call the man. After all you saved his life."

"After he saved mine. I'm sure he wants to forget that piece of his life. It's probably bad enough that he has visual scars to remind him, he doesn't need to hear from me to bring it all up again." What else would they have to talk about? The accident was the one thing that would always define their time together. She wished it wasn't so, but hoping for something didn't make it happen.

"I guess you're right. I hadn't thought about it like that. How are you doing dealing with it, by the way?"

"I'm okay." *When I'm busy enough not to think about it. Which is hardly ever.*

"That's good to hear. Everything happened so fast that it felt like we never really got to say goodbye."

Brooke felt the same way. And not just with Janet and the others at New Hope. But Gareth had been in a coma. Did he know what she had said to him? Did he even know she'd been there? *Does he know why I wasn't there when he woke up?* Since he never called her, she assumed not. And also figured he . . . didn't want to.

"Well, if Alex says yes, the next time I leave Tabiq it won't be in such a rush."

"Speaking of rush, I have to go. I pulled together a staff meeting, and we're talking about changing some of the activities here. Can you believe it, they are getting rid of karaoke?"

"Really. Why?"

Janet chuckled. "If you ask Vinny, it is because they heard me sing. But actually the interest has declined."

"For the entire resort?" That wouldn't be good.

"Yes. I'm not sure why. It was like someone slammed us and we haven't figured out who. But I'm sure the Hendersons will figure it out, and we'll be back on track."

That didn't make any sense to her. A month ago the place was jamming. Why would it change that quickly? They had a wonderful reputation. "I hope they do quickly. I'd hate to think of New Hope closing."

Janet added in a serious tone. "I think it would crush the Hendersons. I'm not sure why, but this place seems to mean more to them than their businesses in the States. They are a wonderful, but odd, family. I don't think I'll ever figure them out."

"The life of the rich, Janet. You can't ever guess what drives their happiness. Sometimes it's something you'd never even think of." *Like the ability to live a normal life traveling as a waitress.*

"I guess you're right. Okay, keep me posted, and good luck when you talk to Alex. I've got my fingers crossed for you."

*Me too. I just don't know what it is I'm wishing for.*

Brooke doubted Alex would say yes based on what Janet mentioned. There would be no benefit in taking her back. But she'd call him in a few days. What did she have to lose? *Not a job. I don't have one right now.*

"What the fuck?" Gareth couldn't believe what he was seeing on the television. That was his face and not a great picture of him either. It was from when he was in the hospital.

REPORTS STATE THAT BILLIONAIRE GARETH LAWSON, WHILE ON A ROMANTIC GETAWAY IN TABIQ WITH BROOKE CORTES, THE DAUGHTER OF BILLIONAIRE TONY CORTES, HAD BEEN SERIOUSLY INJURED DURING AN ALTERCATION AFTER MS. CORTES THREW HER DRINK IN ANOTHER MAN'S FACE. MR. LAWSON WAS IN A COMA AND HAD TO BE LIFEFLIGHTED BACK TO THE STATES WHERE HE CONTINUES TO RECOVER. MS. CORTES AND HER FAMILY, FEARING RETALIATION, HAVE RELOCATED OUTSIDE OF THE UNITED STATES. NEITHER PARTY WERE AVAILABLE FOR COMMENT.

"Gareth, normally I'd remind you to watch your language around Penelope, but actually, those would be my words as well. What is that all about?" Rosslyn asked as she poured him another cup of coffee.

"I'm not sure," he growled. "It's not based on any facts."

"Not from what you told us," Charles said. "But then again, you did leave out the fact you were with the daughter of Tony Cortes."

"Because I didn't fu—I didn't know. Hell, Charles, I'm not sure that's any more real than the rest of the bull they just stated. Why would she be working as a waitress in Tabiq?"

"Like I said, the daughter of Tony Cortes. He's been known to plant people in order to take down a business. He's your average guy in person, but he's ruthless in business. If Brooke is his daughter, she had to be sent there to fu—mess with the Hendersons."

His mind was racing. There was no way sweet Brooke was there to take down anyone. But it was simple enough to know who she was. Gareth pulled out his cell phone and searched Tony Cortes, photos. Sure enough there was one with his wife and daughter. *I can't believe it.*

Everything she said about traveling, wanting to see the world, experience new cultures, was a lie. Brooke really was a spy for her father? That was almost inconceivable. He'd have defended her honor to anyone, even his brothers, because she seemed so genuine. How the hell was he so blind? And not just him, but the Hendersons too. They hired her. *Fuck. I brought her into Alex's home.* He was pissed. Not just at Brooke, but at himself as well.

"Charles, we have to let them know," Gareth said.

"No, we don't. We agreed the best thing we can do as a family, is *not* to work or be close with anything Henderson," Charles stated.

"That was before we learned everything." Before he spent time with Alex and Ziva. "I can't sit back and let them get blindsided."

"I'm sure someone out there will have seen this stupid gossip show that my wife likes to watch in the morning.

They'll figure it out. And if the rumors are correct, the Cortes family is in hiding. Which by the way, if they did just fu— mess with the Hendersons, was a wise thing to do."

Gareth wanted to protect his cousins, but he also needed to see Brooke. He wanted to look her in the face and ask her what the fuck was the truth. Had she only been using him to get closer to the Hendersons? Was that why, after the accident, she was gone? Since she never reached out to him afterward, it was the only thing that made sense.

*The Hendersons can deal with Tony. I'm going to handle Brooke myself.*

"Charles, whether you like it or not, I'm going to Tabiq. We can either join forces and become a stronger family despite the past, or we can hold on to it and let it drive all our future endeavors. Personally, I think both families have a lot to offer each other, professionally and personally. Now if you'll excuse me, I'm going to pack. And by the way, I'm taking the Lawson jet this time."

*Because when I'm done in Tabiq, I'm going to find Brooke.*

"Gareth, remember what I said, you don't have to do this alone."

He turned back to Charles. "You're right, I don't have to, but I choose to. Besides, they weren't talking about you on the TV. It was *my* name linked to the Cortes family. This has gotten personal."

"And if you're not careful, the next accident might not be an accident. A man like Cortes won't stand by quietly and let you fuck with his daughter," Charles said. Rosslyn shot him a look and shook her head. "Sweetheart, I'm trying to make a point."

Rosslyn said, "Then may I help? Maybe I can be a voice of reason here."

Both men stopped and knew it was wise to at least hear her out. There would be hell to pay if they didn't.

"Gareth, you're basing everything on what the TV just said, am I correct?"

"She's Tony's daughter. That is fact."

"Okay. Did she avoid talking to you about her family or her life?" Rosslyn asked.

"No. But then again she didn't tell me she was his daughter either."

"Is it possible that Brooke could've been in Tabiq doing exactly what she said she was doing there? Because if she wasn't, why would she have been the one to call Dylan and tell him about you being in the hospital? Why wouldn't she have let the doctor or some staff member call him? To me, that sounds more like a woman who cared deeply for you, and because of that, she opened herself up to whatever tongue lashing Dylan gave her. And from what I understand, it wasn't very nice. Don't worry, I gave him a piece of my mind about it too."

That just confused shit even more. Rosslyn was right, Brooke could've taken the easy way out. But if she did care about him, that didn't mean she wasn't in Tabiq at her father's request. "You're right, Rosslyn, I need to talk to her. Ask some questions. And let her explain. There's more to the story, and I need to know what it is."

"Gareth, before you go on the attack, you should also take a minute and think about why you never called her," Rosslyn added.

"Is this one of those women always stick together things?" Gareth asked.

Rosslyn put her hands on her hips. "Do you really think I'd stand by someone who intentionally hurt my family?" Gareth shook his head. "Good, because if she isn't who *I* think she is, she won't have to worry about the Hendersons. I'll have a chat with her myself."

Gareth almost laughed. Rosslyn wasn't intimidating in the least, but when her mother-hen instinct kicked in, her demeanor changed. "Okay, I'll think long and hard about my own actions on the flight to Tabiq. Is that acceptable?"

Rosslyn huffed. "It's better, but you have a long way to go before it's acceptable."

Gareth shot Charles a look. *Good luck with this one. She's tougher than you.*

"You two know how to reach me if anything comes up." Gareth knew if he didn't leave now, Rosslyn was going to keep lecturing him on what he was doing incorrectly. He didn't need anyone to tell him he'd made mistakes with Brooke. She was right; he could've called her. The doctor's had told him if she hadn't been there, applied direct pressure to his wound, he probably would've bled out.

*Guess if I was dead, I wouldn't be worried if what I thought we shared was true or not.*

Going back to Tabiq was something he'd already decided to do, even before that stupid shit on TV. All that had done was provide him an explanation to his family. He didn't bring up that his trip was also damage control. Charles didn't want the Lawson name linked to the Hendersons in a negative way, but the same people who came up with that crap could possibly accuse Gareth of helping her and working with Cortes. That would fucking rip Lawson Steel's reputation apart. They wouldn't have to worry about expanding their global business; they'd be out of business.

The flight to Tabiq was far more comfortable in their private jet. It provided much-needed time to think through how to approach the situation. He contemplated calling Alex and letting him know he was coming. But he saved that for when the jet landed. The Hendersons already knew about anyone coming to Tabiq, especially by plane.

"Hi, Alex, guess who is back?"

Alex asked, "Alone or did you bring Brooke with you?"

"Alone. I'm hoping to meet with you. Are you home right now?" The sooner he addressed this, the better. He felt confident that he and Alex could sort this out and come up with a plan so the rumors didn't go any further than they already had.

"I am, and your timing is perfect. Do you need someone to pick you up or can you find your way?"

"I can find your house. I'll be there in about thirty." He ended the call. There was no reason to take any bags off the jet. He believed he was staying, but right now, there was no guarantee on that. All depended on how this meeting went.

*Might be a very short stay in Tabiq.*

It wasn't long before he pulled up to their house. Alex failed to mention he was hosting some sort of party. He was tempted to call back and change the plan, but he was already there, and Gareth knew the security cameras had already announced his arrival.

He had no intention of staying long and didn't want to risk getting boxed in. He parked the loaner vehicle on the street and walked up the driveway. Even before he had a chance to knock, Ziva was opening the door. She gave him a hug then stepped back, wide-eyed.

"I'm sorry. I didn't hurt you, did I? You look so good that I forgot about your back and shoulder."

"It's going to take a lot more than a hug to hurt me," Gareth joked. The fact was, he still was in recovery, and the doctors had a list of things he shouldn't do. Lifting anything heavy topped the list. Since he wasn't planning on visiting the gym, there shouldn't be anything to worry about, health wise that was. "I'm not interrupting anything, am I?"

"You couldn't have come at a better time."

"And why is that?" he asked.

"They are all here. All the Hendersons. This is the first time that has happened since . . . well let's see . . . I think it was my wedding."

"Nope. It was my wedding to Drake. You must be Gareth. I'm Isa, Ziva's sister. Glad you could join us."

The two definitely looked alike. He didn't know Ziva had a sister. Then again, there was a lot he hadn't looked into. When he first started digging, it was only about the Henderson men, not their wives. Before he could respond, yet another woman joined them.

"You're both wrong. It was my wedding to Caydan. I can't believe you two have forgotten that already. Hi, I'm Allyson, one of the many sisters-in-law here. Hope you're hungry because we are about to eat. My husband is manning the grill. He says that is his excuse not to have to chase after all these kids."

Gareth didn't remember a Caydan Henderson. Yet another piece of the puzzle. It seemed there were more secrets in the Henderson family than Alex had let on. *And our secrets are what we need to protect right now.*

"I really can come back another time," Gareth said, but it was too late.

Ziva had grabbed him by the arm and started pulling him inside. "It seems overwhelming at first, but you're from a large family too, so I'm sure you're used to this."

When they arrived in the backyard, Gareth wished he'd come at another time. Kids were running everywhere; it really was a family reunion. He didn't belong there. If he doubted that, the look Brice gave him said it all.

Brice walked over before Gareth could get anywhere close to the rest of the family. In a low tone he said, "What the hell are you doing here?"

"I didn't realize you were having a party." *Alex seemed to have intentionally left that out.*

"I don't mean at the party. I mean back in Tabiq," Brice snarled.

Gareth wasn't intimidated by Brice the first time they met, and just because he was there with the entire Henderson clan, he still wasn't. "I came to speak to Alex. Unless we need your permission, in which case I say, fuck you."

Brice clenched his fist but didn't swing. Gareth knew he wouldn't. No matter how much he might resent that Gareth and Alex had gone behind his back, he wouldn't do anything with all the kids around.

"This is far from over."

"I know. That's why I'm here, because you need my help."

Brice laughed. "I think you've done enough already. I heard. The last time we spoke, we were going to make sure our names were never linked. Getting injured on Tabiq drew a hell of a lot of attention."

"That has yet to be seen. But I was talking about Tony Cortes. Is it true? Is he out to snag New Hope?" Gareth asked.

"He can try. It won't happen. We won't let it. Alex said he told you everything about what had taken place here. We are not allowing any outside companies to come in and prey on these people again. Is that what you came to tell Alex? Because a quick phone call could've saved you a trip."

"You're awfully cocky for a man who hired his daughter," Gareth snapped.

"We knew exactly who she was. As I said, *everyone* who enters Tabiq has a full background check. That includes you."

Coming from anyone else, he'd think it was a bluff. Brice wasn't that guy. Gareth wasn't offended or shocked. After all, he'd done the same exact thing to each Henderson. *Guess we're both assholes.*

"So you knew who she was and hired her anyway? I don't get it. Why expose your business and Tabiq to a potential takeover?"

"Because she's not that person. Brooke is exactly who she said she was."

"A waitress? Her father's a billionaire, and she waits tables. Why?" Gareth asked.

Brice looked at him, "That's something you should ask her yourself."

He planned on it. *Once I know where the hell she is.* "So what are we going to do about these rumors?"

"Nothing," Brice replied.

Gareth arched a brow. "You don't think people are going to start asking questions about what I was doing in Tabiq? And when they do, they are going to find out what a strong presence the Hendersons have here."

"Gareth, we weren't hiding. If so, it'd be hard to run a resort. The only thing we were hoping to keep private was . . . our relationship. Which *you* put at risk for getting out."

Great. He had to hear it from Charles and Brice. Being told he fucked up was getting old. No one seemed to have a resolution to the problem. "So what do you suggest?"

"I gave you mine a year ago. It's your turn to come up with one now," Brice replied.

There was only one option as far as he was concerned. "Do business with Lawson Steel."

"That's not going to happen. It'll put us under a lot of scrutiny."

"Publicly. Full disclosure. You buy it, and we build it. Hell, Brice, it's not like you're going with someone who uses substandard material. Why would anyone question teaming up with the best?" It was now in Brice's hands to decide. Gareth was taking a gamble, but he knew that was the best pitch. It also was a win for both families. Although, perhaps Gareth should've discussed that with his brothers first. Then again, it didn't appear that Brice was doing any differently. Time was of the essence, and they could sort out all the details later.

"You're not just the playboy everyone thinks you are, are you?" Brice asked.

"None of us are what we seem to be. So, do we have a deal or not?" Gareth asked.

"We do. Now, why don't you come with me and let me introduce you to all your . . . *business* partners."

None of them were willing to use the word cousin. As far as they were concerned, it didn't exist in their vocabulary. That didn't mean it wasn't time to start acting more like family. That meant the next stop for Gareth was Panama. He needed to pay Tony Cortes a visit personally.

*Like Rosslyn said, no one fucks with my family.*

Gareth ended up staying the night with the Hendersons before fueling his jet to finish this little *business* trip. He'd thought Brooke would be his next stop, but he needed to make sure her dear ole dad wasn't going to be a problem.

Finding Tony in Panama wasn't difficult at all. But driving up to his home wasn't so easy. It was surrounded by a high wall and a massive gate. To get through, he needed to stop and speak with the armed guard. All of this should be an indication that coming alone was unwise. But he wasn't about to turn around now. He gave the guard his name and waited to see if he'd be allowed inside.

Several minutes later the guard returned and opened the gates. "Proceed to the main building. You will be escorted from there."

Was it a good or bad thing that Tony Cortes seemed to know who he was? *I'm about to find out.* Gareth did as instructed, mostly because he wanted to get out of there alive, after being searched by armed guards for any weapons. He wasn't there to kill Cortes, just to set things straight. Of course, Cortes might not appreciate his visit.

Once inside the home, he was told to wait in a large elaborate marble library with statues of what Gareth assumed to be famous authors. Who knew? To Gareth, this place was gaudy. There was nothing there that reminded him in any way of sweet Brooke.

*No wonder you'd rather wait tables. Beats the hell out of living in this prison.*

He didn't need to wait long before the door opened and Tony entered. Tony didn't look fierce, but then again, Tony was known for having others do his dirty work. Gareth believed if you wanted something done, do it yourself. And that's why he was there.

"I have to admit, I'm surprised to see you here, Mr. Lawson."

"There are a few things I think you and I should discuss in person," Gareth said.

"And what exactly would they be?" Tony asked.

"Let's start with the Hendersons. It has been rumored you might be looking at some of their businesses."

"I don't make it a habit to discuss my business with strangers," Tony said flatly.

"Don't worry. I'm not here to discuss it. I'm here to tell you to keep your hands off anything Henderson or Lawson."

Tony's jaw clenched and he said, "You are a very foolish young man if you think you can come into my home and tell me what I can and can't fucking do. Give me one fucking reason why I shouldn't have my guards escort you off my property immediately?"

*And dealt with. Yeah. I get it.* "Because I'm in love with your daughter and have every intention of marrying her. You can either accept my terms, or I tell her exactly what a fucking piece of shit her father really is and what you really do for a living." It wasn't an empty threat. But he was gambling on how much Brooke meant to her father.

Tony stood, and Gareth swore he saw the veins in his neck pulsing. "I could very easily make it so my daughter never fucking sees or hears from you again; you do know that, don't you?"

Gareth didn't get up and forced himself to remain in control. "You could. But your daughter loves me, and I love her. If you don't care about her happiness, do whatever you fucking want. But since you have allowed her to live her life as she chooses all these years, the life that makes her happy, I suspect she means everything to you."

Tony glared at him long and hard. In a half growl he said, "I don't like you, Lawson."

"You don't have to. This is all about one person. Brooke."

Gareth could tell from the look in Tony's eyes he'd called it right. The only way to get Tony's respect was to show him he was willing to do whatever it took to not just make Brooke happy, but to keep her safe. That meant having balls big enough to stand up to Tony.

"She hasn't told me of your upcoming nuptials. Why is that?" Tony inquired.

"Because I haven't asked her. I figured it was best we come to an understanding first."

Tony smirked. "You have a very unique way of asking for her hand in marriage."

"I take that as a yes?" Gareth asked.

"As long as you understand, this is the last time you enter my home and try to muscle me."

Great. He just got the blessing to be a member of yet another family filled with fucking secrets.

Brooke stood on the beach watching the sunrise. She couldn't help but think about the last time she was in this exact spot. It had been the beginning of the best day of her life. Gareth had swept her off her feet for the most romantic getaway.

Gareth, a man of such wealth, really seemed to understand her. She didn't want loud and flashy. If she did, she could have stayed living with her parents. Glitz and glam. A total turn off for her. She saw beauty in simplicity.

She thought by coming back to New Hope, she'd find peace. She was wrong. It actually was worse than any place she'd been. Everything reminded her of Gareth: the lobby, the halls, the beach. But Brooke had practically begged for her old job back. How could she go to Alex and tell him she made a mistake?

That was it. She had to suck it up and follow through. She owed it to them and also to herself. She wasn't a quitter. Eventually the pain of being without Gareth would subside. She closed her eyes and released another heavy sigh. *If I don't die of a broken heart first.*

She heard a splash in the water and stepped closer. Someone was swimming. Might it be? Had Gareth come back to Tabiq? Could they replay their time together, but this time with a happy ending? She looked closer and could tell it was a man in the water, and he was swimming to shore.

Her heart raced in anticipation. What would she say? How could she explain not calling him? Not being there when he woke? She'd thought it was the best thing for him and his family, but it sure as hell hadn't been the best for her. It was pure hell wondering each moment how he was doing but not knowing. When she accepted that she'd been wrong in not going to the States with him, it was too late. Too much time had passed. He'd woken up and found her gone.

She wanted their paths to cross again. Had she come here hoping against hope they would? But now that he was heading her way, she was . . . wasn't ready. But she couldn't turn and make her escape up the beach and duck back into the hotel. A couple more strokes then he stood and walked toward her. *You can do this, Brooke. It's what you wanted. Just . . . not how you pictured it.*

So she stood watching, anticipating as the waves crashed upon her toes. As he drew closer, she knew he wasn't Gareth. The man was fit, but she had kissed and nibbled every inch of Gareth and his body was etched permanently in her mind. *The only place he exists.*

"Good morning," she said as the guest walked past her. He nodded and quickly continued on his way. That was fine with her. She wasn't in the mood for small talk. Actually, she felt more like crying. Her heart was so heavy. "Gareth, why didn't I tell you when I had the chance?" she whispered.

"What would you have said?" a voice asked from behind her.

She spun around to find Gareth holding a bouquet of gardenias. "Gareth. You're here?"

"Yes. And wanting to know what you wished you had told me." He stepped closer, now only inches away.

168

"I . . . I . . ." she stammered, not sure how to say it. They were the three little words she ached to say, but he deserved more. "Gareth, how are you doing?"

"I'm good. Healed for the most part. But that's not why I'm here."

"Why are you here?" She felt like a coward putting this on him. She knew how she felt. She'd told him each night as she looked at the stars.

"I'm here to see you," Gareth stated.

"How did you know I was back?" Alex had to have told him.

"Would you believe me if I said your father told me?"

*My father? No.* "You called my father?"

"No. I went and saw him."

"In Panama?" That made no sense. Why would he do that?

"Not my kind of place, but yes, in Panama."

She had spoken to her parents last night, and neither of them mentioned anything about Gareth visiting them. "Were you there on vacation?"

"No."

He wasn't making it easy for her. Then again, she hadn't answered his question either. Maybe she needed to ask the right questions.

"Did you go to talk about me?" That was pretty clear.

"I did."

*And that's not much better.* "About what?" How could he avoid that one?

"Us."

*Really?* "Gareth, just tell me why you were there. What you talked about."

"Hmm. Why don't you tell me what you wished you had said before?" Gareth asked with a wicked grin.

*Well played.* "Fine. I would've told you that . . . that I love you." There. She said it. Her stomach was doing flips and she waited, hoping to hear those words back. All he did was smile. Maybe he didn't love her back. He'd made it clear he enjoyed his carefree bachelor life. *But I changed. I thought maybe you did too.* "Now I believe it's your turn to answer me. Why did you go see my father?"

He stepped even closer. "To tell him that I love you, and I want to marry you."

"You . . . you . . . what?"

"You know, the old-fashioned, ask your father for your hand in marriage thing. I'm hoping this is where you say yes."

She blinked and wondered if this was all a dream. Her father was one tough man when it came to men in her life. No one went to speak to him, definitely not willingly. Yet Gareth went there on his own and actually came out in one piece. Should she be impressed or scared?

"Brooke, are you going to answer me?" he asked.

"Gareth, I'm . . . you're . . . sure about this, right? I mean . . . there is so much you don't know about me."

"And so much you don't know about me either. But if you say yes, we'll have a lifetime to find out." He stroked her cheek with the back of his hand. "Brooke, until I met you, I never thought I'd want to settle down."

"I know. You told me. That's why I . . . I don't know why you're asking me to marry you now."

"Sometimes you don't know you're missing something in your life, until you have it. And once you have it, you can't picture being without it. For me, that is you, Brooke. Home is not the walls that surround us. It's a feeling you carry inside. For me, home is waking with you in my arms every day. Whether it's here, back in New York, or in Panama, I want to be where you are. Brooke, I'm not asking you to give up your life, I'm asking to be part of it."

Her hands trembled, her legs wobbled, and her stomach fluttered. "Gareth, can you . . . will you . . . ask me again please?"

Gareth reached out to take her hand in his and dropped down on one knee. "Brooke Cortes, would you do me the honor of marrying me so we can spend the rest of our lives laughing, loving, and learning all about each other?"

"Gareth, no one can make me laugh like you do, and I have never felt so loved. Yes, I'll marry you."

Gareth rose, dropped the flowers on the ground, and scooped her into his arms. She felt him wince as he kissed her. She loved the feel of his lips on hers, but she also felt how tense his body was.

Breaking their sweet reunion, she said, "Gareth, put me down." He let her slide down him and back into the cool water. "You're . . . hurting, aren't you?"

"The only thing that would've hurt is if you had said no."

She placed her hands on his chest. "If I'm going to be your wife, you might as well start telling me the truth. Are you okay?"

He shook his head. "I'm not supposed to be lifting anything more than ten pounds until I see the doctor again."

"And you picked me up? Are you crazy?" she blurted.

He laughed. "I've been crazy about you since the first time I saw you." Gareth pulled her even closer. "And when you kiss me like that, I freaking lose my mind."

"So, you're saying this is all my fault?" she teased.

"Absolutely. You stole my heart and won't give it back. Now you're stuck with me."

Brooke smiled and stood on her tippy toes, wrapping her arms around his neck. "I hate to deliver bad news, but I'm holding your heart hostage. We can negotiate its return in about seventy years from now."

Gareth laughed "I'll be one hundred three by then."

"Hmm. Do you know studies show a healthy, active sex life can actually add years to your life?"

"Really? I have no problem living to be one hundred fifty if it's with you. But I think we should start working on it now. What do you say?"

Brooke said, "Okay, but until you get the all clear from the doctor—"

"Don't you dare say we can't make love," Gareth warned.

Brooke snickered. "I was going to say, I'll be on top." She pulled him closer and said, "And I say we shoot for one seventy-five."

The moment their lips made contact, she knew it was no dream. Dreams didn't come as sweet at that. She'd come to Tabiq to learn about a culture, but in actuality, Tabiq had taught her more about herself. She hadn't been searching, she'd been running. And for the first time in her life, she wasn't dreaming of what came next. Because she had everything she could possible want.

# EPILOGUE

If anyone had told him this day would come, he'd have told them they were nuts. Lawson Steel had always been his life. But it was time for a change, and this was it. He was branching out on his own. Well, not totally. Brooke was by his side.

"I can't believe you're really doing this. You never said how you came up with the name of the company," Charles inquired.

"This journey all started because of a secret, so I figured since the secrets are out, why not call my company, The Answer."

"It's actually genius. You sure you don't want to reconsider?"

That wasn't going to happen. The paperwork was complete, and he already had his first client waiting for him. Gareth was moving forward and not stopping until he made Brooke proud. "You guys don't need me taking up office space," Gareth replied.

"You underestimate your value to the company," Charles

said seriously. "Just remember, you'll always be part of Lawson Steel, even if you're not working here."

"Thanks, Charles. It's been a good run." *I hope for as much success with the next one.*

"I have to admit, I never would've thought you'd start your own construction company. I know I'm out of the loop on some things, but what exactly brought all this on?"

He wasn't going to explain the little mishap in the kitchen at New Hope, but that had been a large piece of it. "I've been thinking about doing this for years. But getting to see what the Hendersons have been doing in Tabiq, made me want to get more hands-on."

"From what you told me, hands-on is exactly what you'll be doing. Are you sure the doctor has cleared you for that type of work? If not, I have a feeling you'll find yourself tied down to a bed and not in a way you're going to enjoy either," Charles teased.

Gareth laughed. It was nice to see his big brother cracking jokes. "Don't worry, Brooke already threatened me. And being tied down to a bed would be gentle compared to what she said. Have you ever noticed women can be so tiny and fragile looking, but do something stupid and they can—"

"Scare the shit out of you?"

Gareth nodded. "Her father is not as intimidating as Brooke is when she's mad."

Charles asked, "Not worried about Tony being your father-in-law some day?"

It was a valid question, one he'd have asked if any of his brothers were about to do the same thing. There was a time when Gareth would've distanced himself, but doing so would hurt Brooke. Tony was her father, and even though Gareth didn't like the way the man did business, they had an understanding, one that he felt Tony would honor. That didn't mean

174

Gareth wouldn't keep his eyes open. Tony wasn't a fool, and he knew the scandal it'd cause for his daughter if he wasn't... careful. Gareth knew Tony would do anything to protect Brooke. *And so would I.* Gareth looked over and saw her parents talking to Alex, Ziva, and a few others of the Henderson clan. The Hendersons knew very well what Tony Cortes was all about, yet there was no sign of any tension between any of them. The one thing they all shared was love of family.

"With everything we've learned about our dear ole great-granddad and his involvement with the corruption in Tabiq"—that was putting it lightly—"I've learned you can't control anyone else's behavior, but you don't have to put up with their shit either. I wish we were around when they were fucking with Tabiq. I'd have loved to straighten their asses out and—"

"Made them pay. In a way, we all have to consider ourselves lucky."

"You mean because most people in this room are descendants of assholes?"

Charles nodded. "We have Mom to thank for our good genes."

"The Hendersons thank Sophie Barrington. Brooke still seems ignorant of her father's business dealings."

"That's sad, because someday that secret will come out."

*They all do in time.* "And I'll be there for her when it does."

"We all will," Charles said. "She's good for you, Gareth."

"Yes, she is." He looked across the room and smiled as he saw Brooke chatting up a storm with Rosslyn. They probably were talking about wedding plans by the look on their faces. He loved seeing her so happy and looked forward to making her smile for years to come. "I can't picture my life without her."

"I know I told you before that going to Tabiq had been a mistake. I was wrong. It was exactly where you needed to go. You found a lot more than the answers we were looking for."

"Yes, I did. When Alex told me what our great-granddad had done, I was so filled with hate. If it wasn't for Brooke being there, it might have consumed me. At one point if I could've changed my last name, I would have."

"What changed your mind?"

Gareth smiled. *Falling in love.* "I learned the past can't be changed, but you have control over the future." *She's mine.*

"I can't agree with you more. There's something Rosslyn and I were going to share later once it was only Lawsons around, but I think Rosslyn will forgive me if I tell you now."

That piqued his interest. He normally wasn't the first to learn of anything. "What's that?" Gareth asked.

"Penelope is going to have a baby brother."

Gareth turned and looked closely at Rosslyn, who didn't look pregnant. "You're serious?"

"I am. She's only nine weeks, but we already know it's a boy."

"So the torch gets passed on," Gareth said. It was bittersweet, but he was happy for Charles.

Charles shook his head. "We're actually naming him after Rosslyn's father. The legacy stops here. There will *not* be a Charles Joseph Lawson the Eighth."

"Fuck yeah! Damn, Charles. I'm not sure if I'm happier about the baby or the name."

"Just remember, no one knows," Charles said in a low voice.

Gareth nodded. "Dad is going to flip."

"Let him. I love Dad, but this is my life. I'm done being

told what I have to do because it is family tradition. We are not like our ancestors, and there is no way in hell I am naming my son after them. Like you said, it's time to make some changes."

"I bet we're going to pave the way for a better future for our children. Well, someday if or when I actually have some." He and Brooke had discussed children, but they were taking one step at a time. They were both young. No need to rush into everything. Although he'd like his children to grow up with their cousins.

"I'm thinking you're going to have the most kids out of all of us."

"Why would you think that?"

Charles laughed. "Because you're the one who said he never wanted any. You're not even married and already talking about them."

"Don't put any money on that bet. Let me start with one first," Gareth laughed.

"You two look like you're in a deep conversation. Anything we should know about?" Dylan asked with Sofia by his side. Seth, Jordan, and Ethan joined them from the porch.

"Charles and I are taking bets on who will have the most children. Do you want in?" Gareth asked. The single brothers looked at one another and seemed to decide to get out while the going was good. Each of them rattled off an excuse why they couldn't stay.

Seth was the last to go, stating, "I just broke free from a lengthy conversation with Charlene on the porch. The last thing I want to do is talk about marriage or children."

Gareth looked closely at Seth before he dashed off. *Rosslyn, could you be right?* He'd never wish that on his brother, but then again, opposites do attract. Seth didn't need settling down, he needed some excitement to shake up his work 24/7 life. *Tread carefully brother, or she'll have a ring on her finger before you even know what hit you.* Gareth decided not to share that warning out loud.

When he turned his attention back to Dylan, who hadn't bolted, he had that look in his eyes that said he was eager to partake. Gareth and Dylan competed in almost everything growing up. This was much different. But before Dylan could respond Sofia said, "Don't you dare play that game! I haven't had this one yet and I know how competitive you are."

Dylan laughed. "Sofia, you know you want a dozen."

"Roses? Maybe. Children? I don't think so," Sofia snorted.

Charles said, "Oh, I might need to change my bet. Dylan is very competitive."

Sofia shook her head. "We are supposed to be here to celebrate The Answer, not to place bets on babies."

"We said congratulations. What else do you want us to do?" Dylan asked.

"Not talk about babies. Maybe we can all talk about the wedding instead," Sofia suggested.

In unison the men all said, "No!"

She laughed. "Fine. Then I'm going to talk with Brooke and Rosslyn. I'm sure their conversation is much more interesting."

Gareth watched as Sofia walked over to Brooke and then pointed in their direction.

"I think we're in trouble," Gareth said.

"What makes you think that?" Charles asked.

"The look on the ladies' faces. Just so you know, I'm blaming you."

Charles asked, "What did I do?"

"You're the oldest. It's your job to keep us in line," Gareth teased.

"Nope. That's what you're getting married for," Charles shot back. "Not that I want details, but how are the wedding plans coming? I thought you'd have a date by now."

He hadn't expected Charles to be asking about the wedding. Usually he was all business. It wasn't like they hadn't just celebrated Dylan's wedding a few months ago. Then again, Rosslyn probably hounded Charles to put the pressure on. "Still ironing out a few things," Gareth said.

Dylan laughed. "You'll still be doing that the day of the wedding. Hell, why can't they just send us a text telling us where to be and when. I think it'd be less stressful for them."

Charles said, "As Rosslyn reminded me several times, it was *our* wedding and wanted to make sure I had everything I wanted. I did. I had her. Nothing else mattered to me. Definitely not scanning through flowers and decorations."

Gareth had to agree. But these weren't things he and Brooke needed to worry about any longer. Both of them wanted to keep it out of the tabloids. That meant keeping it low-key. At least they were on the same page as to what they wanted. Hopefully everyone they loved would accept that.

Charles had shared some private information, and he wished he could do the same. But Gareth had promised they would make their announcement together. This was the perfect venue to do so. Everyone was there. Her parents, his parents, all his siblings and even all their new found family, the Hendersons with their spouses were in attendance. That might be what had shocked him the most. When he asked Brice why all the Hendersons had shown up, besides the fact they were invited, Brice informed him they were family and family supported each other through both the good and bad times. It was going to take some getting used to, not looking at the Hendersons and wondering what they were hiding and just looking at them as family that had their back.

Gareth couldn't help but wonder if any of this would've been possible if Alex hadn't been so forthcoming. Gareth knew eventually it'd all have come out, but the trust wouldn't have been there. Not like it was today, which had made their presence all the more important.

But with so many in attendance, Brooke had been talking with everyone else and not once had they actually been together long enough to do it. *Sometimes you have to make things happen.*

"If you'll excuse me, I'm going to check on Brooke." He left his brothers and went up to Brooke and asked, "Hi, can I talk to you for a minute?"

She smiled and said, "Of course. If you ladies will excuse me for a minute, this handsome man wants to steal me away."

Rosslyn laughed. "Don't steal her too far. We're planning the wedding and we're just about to talk dresses."

"She won't be gone long," Gareth promised as he guided her to a more private spot.

"Your timing was perfect. They were asking so many questions, and I didn't want to start lying to them. They kept asking if we set a date yet. I thought for sure they were going to pick one for us."

He felt bad because he'd been running late, and she probably was wondering what had happened to their plan. The problem about getting together for a social event, when you also work with one another, was trying not to talk business. They failed every time. But for the most part, they kept the conversations on family. On the future. Both fitting for today.

He took Brooke's hand and softly asked, "Are you sure you still want to do this?"

"Of course I am. You know me, I love surprises."

Gareth pulled her close. "Don't look at me like that or

you'll get one. I'll scoop you up right now and carry you away."

"Don't you dare," she warned. Then he watched Brooke as she looked around at everyone in the room. She was smiling, and he knew this was right. When she turned back to him she added, "It's time to surprise everyone else."

"Okay." He nodded to one of the waiters who had been brought into the loop. The waiter left the room and the soft music was turned off. *Here it goes.*

A man approached and stood between them. In a loud voice he said, "May I have everyone's attention please."

The room was loud with everyone's chatter and laughter. He hated to do it, but he needed them to quiet down. This wasn't going to take long, but he needed them to cooperate. So Gareth put two fingers to his lips and let out a loud high-pitched whistle. Finally, one by one, they quieted and turned. "Brooke and I wanted to thank you all for coming out tonight to celebrate The Answer. We appreciate all the love and support you've given us these past few months. And we look forward to beginning the next chapter of our lives."

Brooke added, "You are all so very special to us. And whether you're family or friends, or a combination of both, you were all invited here because we didn't want to do this without you. You weren't just invited to a party, but to witness our wedding."

The room all started to buzz, and the looks on their faces said they definitely were not expecting this. Gareth looked to Charles, who had a smile on his face, then to Tony, who shockingly nodded his approval. There didn't seem to be one guest upset with the change of plans. That's good, because they were going ahead with it no matter what.

As on cue, the waiter opened the door and he and other staff carried in the wedding arch decorated with white gardenias, the flower that would forever be a symbol of his love for Brooke. One of the waitresses handed Brooke a matching bouquet. She might not be in a traditional wedding dress, but she was still the most beautiful bride he'd ever seen. *And I'm the luckiest man alive.*

Gareth looked around the room and said, "Dylan, if you don't mind, I believe you owe me." He waved for Dylan to come stand beside him.

Dylan walked over and shook Gareth's hand. "We'll talk about this later."

It hadn't been easy keeping this from all of them. But Brooke said she wanted something private and simple. Her happiness was all that mattered.

Brooke then called out, "Janet, I need you here." Janet made her way through the crowd of family and gave Brooke a hug. "You said I'd find my *real love* someday. You were right. Will you stand by me as my matron of honor?"

"I'd love to."

The room became quiet again as Brooke and Gareth turned to face each other. At Dylan's wedding, he couldn't concentrate on anything but missing Brooke. Here he was now, about to marry the most amazing woman he'd ever met. Luck had nothing to do with it. Fate brought them together and love was going to make it last. He leaned over and whispered, "I love you."

Her eyes glistened and she said, "I love you too."

The judge said, "We are gathered together, friends and family, to join this man and this woman in holy matrimony. What their love has bound together, let nothing tear apart . . .

*Till death do us part. I love you, my Brooke. And I always will . . .*

## The End

## When Sparks Fly Series:

Drive Me Wild

Plug Me In

Turn Me On

\*\*\*\*\*\*\*\*\*\*\*\*\*\*\*\*\*\*\*\*\*\*\*\*\*\*\*\*\*\*\*\*\*\*\*\*\*\*\*\*\*\*\*\*\*\*\*\*\*\*\*\*\*\*\*

## The Blank Check Series:

Book 1: The Billionaire's Rival

Book 2: The Billionaire's Charade

Book 3: The Billionaire's Scandal

Book 4: The Billionaire's Regret

Book 5: The Billionaire's Deception

Book 6: The Billionaire's Revenge

### *The Billionaire's Rival*

Charles Lawson carries the weight of the entire family's future on his shoulders. As CEO of Lawson Steel it is his responsibility to ensure their legacy continued for the next generation. First on his agenda is to clean up loose ends from the past. Doing so is risky and if he fails, the price could be great. It's a risk he's willing to take.

Rosslyn Clark loves her life as is, but family is everything to her. When her parents find themselves in a crisis, all she loves is at risk. Whether she likes it or not, sometimes change is inevitable.

As Charles prepares to seal the deal, he finds one beautiful blonde stands in his way, and things become complicated. Can he continue with his original plan and look at her as collateral damage or has Rosslyn become something more to him?

Rosslyn finds herself caught between two powerful men, one she works for, the other, his rival. Will she do what is expected of her, or will she walk away from everything and follow her heart?

\*\*\*\*\*\*\*\*\*\*\*\*\*\*\*\*\*\*\*\*\*\*\*\*\*\*\*\*\*\*\*\*\*\*\*\*\*\*\*\*\*\*\*\*\*\*\*\*\*\*\*\*

### Barrington Billionaires Series:

Book 1: One White Lie (FREE!)

Book 2: Table For Two

Book 3: You & Me Make Three

Book 4: Virgin For The Fourth Time

Book 5: His For Five Nights

Book 5.5: New Beginning Holiday Novella

Book 6: After Six

Book 7: Seven Guilty Pleasures

Book 7.5: At the Sight of Holly

Book 8: Eight Reasons Why

Book 9: Nine Rules of Engagement

### *One White Lie*

Brice Henderson traded everything for power and success. His company was closing a deal that would cement his spot at the top. The last thing he needed was a distraction from the past.

Lena Razzi had spent years trying to forget Brice Henderson. When offered the opportunity of a lifetime, would she take the risk even if the price would be another broken heart?

Do you love reading from this world? Continue with Always Mine from my sister, Ruth Cardello, Her series will mirror my time line. It isn't necessary to read hers to enjoy mine, but it sure will enhance the fun!

\*\*\*\*\*\*\*\*\*\*\*\*\*\*\*\*\*\*\*\*\*\*\*\*\*\*\*\*\*\*\*\*\*\*\*\*\*\*\*\*\*\*\*\*\*\*\*\*\*\*\*\*\*\*

### **Betting on You Series:**

Book 1: The Billionaire's Secret (FREE!)

Book 2: The Billionaire's Masquerade

Book 3: The Billionaire's Longshot

Book 4: The Billionaire's Jackpot

Book 5: All Bets Off

Book 6: A Rose For The Billionaire

Book 7: The Billionaire's Treat Novella

#### *The Billionaire's Secret*

Billionaire Jon Vinchi is a man with one passion: work. His friends decide to shake him up by entering him as a prize at a charity event.

Accountant Lizette Burke is dressed to the nines and covering for her boss at a charity event. She's hoping to land a donor for the struggling non-profit agency that employs her.

She never expected to win a date with a billionaire.

He never thought one night could turn his life upside down.

One lie stands between them and their happily ever after. Too bad it's a big one!

\*\*\*\*\*\*\*\*\*\*\*\*\*\*\*\*\*\*\*\*\*\*\*\*\*\*\*\*\*\*\*\*\*\*\*\*\*\*\*\*\*\*\*\*\*\*\*\*\*\*\*\*\*\*

## **Southern Desires Series:**

Book 1: Southern Spice (FREE!)

Book 2: Southern Exposure

Book 3: Southern Delight

Book 4: Southern Regions

Book 5: Southern Charm

Book 6: Southern Sass

Novella: Southern Hearts

### *Southern Spice*

Derrick Nash knows the pain of loss. But is he seeking justice or revenge? He doesn't care as long as someone pays the price.

It is Casey Collin's duty at FEMA to help those in need when a natural disaster strikes. After a tornado hits Honeywell, she finds there are more problems than just storm damage. Will she follow company procedures or her heart?

Can Derrick move forward without the answers he's been searching for? Can Casey teach him how to trust again? Or will she need to face the fact that not every story has a happy ending?

\*\*\*\*\*\*\*\*\*\*\*\*\*\*\*\*\*\*\*\*\*\*\*\*\*\*\*\*\*\*\*\*\*\*\*\*\*\*\*\*\*\*\*\*\*\*\*\*\*\*\*\*

## Turchetta's Promise Series:

Book 1: For Honor (FREE!)

Book 2: For Hope

Book 3: For Justice

Book 4: For Truth

Book 5: For Passion

Book 6: For Love

Book 7: For Keeps

### *For Honor*

Looking for a new Romantic Intrigue? Then you will love the Turchetta's. You met them in both the Betting On You Series as well as Barrington Billionaires Series. Now it is time for an up close look into their lives.

Rafe Turchetta may have retired from the Air Force, but his life was still dedicated to fighting the injustice of the world. There was one offense that went so wrong, and it will haunt him, as it continues to destroy him on the inside.

Deanna Glenn was being tortured by a tragedy, one that she couldn't share with anyone. Time was running out and she needed the lies to cease before she started to believe them herself.

Healing meant returning to where it all went horribly wrong years ago. For Deanna she needed to take on a new identity. For Rafe, that meant doing whatever he needed to in order to get her to speak the truth.

When danger rears its ugly head will Rafe follow his heart and protect Deanna even if it means never learning the truth? Or will Deanna sacrifice her happiness and expose it all?

*Books by Ruth Cardello*

ruthcardello.com

*Books by Danielle Stewart*

authordaniellestewart.com

Do you like sweet romance? You might enjoy Lena Lane

www.lenalanenovels.com

BY JEANNETTE WINTERS & LENA LANE

Muse and Mayhem Series

Book 1: The Write Appeal

Book 2: The Write Bride

Book 3: The Write Connection(2019)

Printed in Great Britain
by Amazon